BOUND AS HIS BUSINESS-DEAL BRIDE

KALI ANTHONY

MILLS & BOON

First published in Great Britain 2020
by Mills & Boon, an imprint of HarperCollins*Publishers*
1 London Bridge Street, London, SE1 9GF

www.harpercollins.co.uk

HarperCollins*Publishers*
1st Floor, Watermarque Building, Ringsend Road
Dublin 4, Ireland

Large Print edition 2021

© 2020 Kali Anthony

ISBN: 978-0-263-28842-1

MIX
Paper from
responsible sources
FSC® C007454

This book is produced from independently certified FSC™ paper to ensure responsible forest management. For more information visit www.harpercollins.co.uk/green.

Printed and bound in Great Britain
by CPI Group (UK) Ltd, Croydon, CR0 4YY

To Philip.
My own romance hero
and happily-ever-after.

PROLOGUE

Then

'ARE YOU HURT?'

Eve shivered as Gage pulled his coat close around her, covering the wet clothes clinging to her body. A cold trickle of rainwater drizzled down her spine from the hair plastered to her head. She reached her hand to her temple, probing the area where a dull throb ached. 'Only a bump, but I'm okay.'

'Where?' Gage's voice sounded urgent. A torch flicked on. She winced as the brightness of it cut through the dark.

'Here.' She touched her head again and his gentle fingers brushed her own out of the way, tracing over her skin where it hurt the most. She shivered again, but not from the cold. This one was something warmer and suffused with pleasure.

'I'm sorry,' he said. His soft lips touched the

middle of her forehead. He bent down and placed the torch on the floor, the small halo of light like a cocoon around them. 'Anywhere else?'

She shook her head. 'What about you?' He'd been driving when they'd slid off the road in the deluge. They'd been in a rush, trying to get away quickly because she was sure her sister, Veronique, had seen her sneak out of the house to meet Gage and run.

'I'm fine,' he said. 'Don't worry about me.'

She searched his face, shadowed as it was by the grim darkness that surrounded them in the abandoned building they'd found after grabbing their packs and fleeing the wrecked car. He looked okay, but he'd never tell if he wasn't. Gage always tried to protect her from every hurt. She wished he'd let her protect him sometimes.

'Did we have to leave the car?'

'It wasn't going anywhere, and we can't drive with that damage. It'll draw attention. At least it's off the road and not a hazard.'

Gage wrapped his arms round her and drew her close. She nestled into his damp chest as rain pattered on the roof above them. In places where the roof wasn't secure water leaked through, pooling on the floor.

'It'll be okay, *cher*. We've got some money.' He squeezed a pocket on the coat she wore. A few thousand dollars wasn't much, but it would get them where they needed to go, she supposed. Gage promised it would, and he always kept his promises. 'We'll hole up here tonight and catch a bus to Montgomery first thing. It's only a few hours away. Then we can get married and no one can stop us. Not your family, not Mom and Dad...'

His voice trailed off as sadness tainted it. Gage loved his parents, but the Caron and the Chevalier families had loathed each other for as long as she and Gage had been alive. His mom and dad had made it clear to him they didn't approve of their relationship, even though he'd tried to convince them that while she was only twenty and he twenty-three, they loved each other and that's all that mattered. It hadn't changed their minds.

As for her family...a knot tightened in her stomach, a sickening ache that had been present for so long she barely noticed it some days. She couldn't think about what would have happened if they'd known. Eve wrapped her arms tightly round Gage's strong torso.

'You're sure about this?' she asked. They might love each other, but he was still losing something by being with her—the support of his family, who were important to him.

Gage pulled back and looked down at her. The pale yellow torchlight bled the colour from his eyes, making them appear greener than the unearthly blue that filled her waking thoughts and dreams for the future. 'I love you. And we don't need anyone's consent to marry in Alabama, not like home.'

If only she'd been twenty-one, they wouldn't have had to run. But they couldn't wait. She was afraid of the parades of eligible suitors her father had forced on her, and what they might mean. Now, with her enrolment in a French finishing school finalised, there was no escaping the truth. It was a choice between running or not seeing each other for a year, maybe longer. No contact at all. The thought was unbearable. She couldn't. It had made the decision easier for her, at least. For Gage, she knew it had cost something more, even though he didn't say so.

Gage ran his hand through his wet hair, his

normal blond darkened by the rain. She couldn't miss the tightness round his eyes, that look of worry present most of the time in recent months. 'You're not having second thoughts, are you?'

'Never.'

He smiled, and it was the most beautiful thing she'd ever seen. The chill dissolved as she was warmed from the inside out. The mere memory of his smile made every day better. Even the ones where even the music turned up too loud at home couldn't drown out her mom and dad's shouting. The days when her mom took to her room, with only her pills and gin-spiked iced tea for company.

Gage cupped her jaw. Dropped his lips to hers. His mouth was so tender and gentle she melted into him, her hands gripping his wet Henley. She needed more than this, kisses in a grimy, falling-down building.

Once they were married they could find a hotel, make love in a proper bed like they had a few weeks before, when they'd sneaked into the guesthouse on his parents' property. It could have been the Waldorf the way he'd treated her like a princess on the crisp, white sheets. A flush of desire flooded through her at the memory of his bare skin slipping over hers. How he'd filled her, body and soul. She'd cried in his arms because he'd made her feel so perfect, at a time where everything had seemed broken.

His tongue touched hers and she threaded her fingers through his hair as they deepened the kiss. She needed him close to her again, craved it in a way she could never explain. He was her everything, the only man she ever wanted. Soon no one could stop them. The thrill of that thought surged through her, the realisation that in a matter of days she'd become Mrs Gage Caron.

He stopped, wrenched away from her and bent down, the loss immediate and shocking. Everything plunged into midnight as the torch was shut off. 'Wha—?'

Gage pressed his finger against her lips. Behind him the ghost of a light flickered, a brief flash in another part of the building. The scrape of something. Shoes on floor? She froze, her heart pounding in her chest like drumsticks, drowning out the sound of anything else. Gage's breath caressed her ear. 'Someone's here.'

His warmth had left her. She didn't know where he was, but he wouldn't leave her alone.

Not ever. She flinched at a rustling sound nearby. As her eyes adjusted to the darkness, she saw him hunched close, stuffing things into his pack.

'Hide,' he whispered, his voice like a mere breath over the sound of rain falling on the roof above them.

'It might not be my father.'

'Can't take that chance.'

'What about you?'

She could barely make out the shake of his head. 'You take the money, head to Montgomery and I'll meet you. Call me when you get there. Now up.'

She looked into the black, ominous rafters above her and hesitated.

'You scared?' Gage asked.

Terrified. But his words lit a fire in her belly. After they'd first met as children, spying each other through an ivy-covered hole in the wall that separated the Chevalier and Caron family estates, he'd ask that whenever she hesitated. She'd never backed down from his challenges, always pretending they hadn't bothered her a bit, even when they had.

'It's just like climbing the old magnolia. Remember?' Gage's face was hidden by the darkness but brittleness cracked in his voice, telling Eve just how scared he was too. Her mouth dried. She nodded, peering into the rafters again.

'I remember.'

She'd never forget sitting in those branches, looking down at the world as if one day they could bend it to their every whim. Her mom would have had a conniption to know her precious baby girl was up a tree, especially with a *filthy Caron*. But with Gage anything had seemed possible, no matter how bad things had been. Up there, in their world of fantasy, trying to shut out real life and touch the sky, had been the place her childhood crush had turned into full-blown love.

Gage bundled some more belongings into his pack. He stuffed hers through a punched-out hole in the wall into the cavity space, out of sight.

'Now's the time to climb like a tiger's on your tail, *cher*,' he whispered. The sounds of the searchers drifted closer. Men's hushed voices. Sniggers.

'Come out, come out, wherever you are.'

Like some sick game. They were hunting and she was the catch of the day. She almost lost her meagre dinner there on the floor, but swallowed down the saliva flooding her mouth. Gage closed the space between them, kissing her again. Not gently this time. His lips were hard and fast against her own, bringing her back to herself. She didn't want to let him go. Not now, not ever.

'I'll get them away from here. Then you run.'

He released her and bent from the waist, clasping his fingers in front of him. She put a foot into his cupped hands, just like when they'd been kids and he'd always helped her into the tree. Gage hoisted her up and she grabbed a rough beam with her bare fingers. Splinters bit into her soft flesh. She clung to the wood, huddled in the darkness as she perched in the old rafters, trying to make herself as small as possible.

She was good at making herself small.

Dim light from the street bled through the dirty, broken windows. Gage gave her a long, last look. Flickers of torchlight came closer. He kissed his fingers and reached them out in her direction.

'Soon.'

He hoisted his pack and crept away quietly till he was almost out of sight. Then he scuffed his trainers on the floor, deliberately making a noise. He was the decoy, like a mother duck leading hunters away from her ducklings. Eve took a deep breath, trying to steady her anxious heartbeat. She had money in her pocket. When Gage and her father's men were gone, she'd swing down somehow and make her way to Montgomery. They'd find each other. Marry like they'd planned. It would be fine.

Shouts.

'There! He's there!'

The pounding of booted feet. A commotion, scuffling. A cacophony of sound she couldn't make out.

'Got him!'

'Let me go!'

Gage's voice, like she'd never heard it. He'd always made her feel safe. Now he sounded as terrified as she felt. She gripped the beam under her so tight it cut into her fingers and she closed her eyes, trying to make out the voices over the rain falling on the roof. She hoped he was just acting, playing it up for the men who'd caught him.

'Where is she?'

Eve froze, stopped breathing, because that voice she knew. *Her father.* There were a few beats of silence then a thud, a grunt. A swift, sharp crack like a snapping twig. Then Gage's voice, thick and broken.

'She's gone.'

Had they hurt him? Eve's breathing burst in quick pants. Her head spun as she tried to stay calm. If she fainted and dropped from her hiding place, everything would be lost.

'She left you?'

'You'll never, ever find her. I've made sure of it.'

She couldn't hear her father's response, only the murmurs of men that became louder and louder. More torchlight, now below her, flicked into the dark corners of the space. She jumped as one man kicked over some dirty crates in his search. He sneezed loudly and she flinched. The disturbed dust tickled her own nose and she held her breath. They couldn't look up. Not up. *Please.*

The rain fell heavier now, beating staccato

on the roof. Another deluge on the way. She strained to hear over the sound of it, which meant the men below would have to as well.

'Nothing, boss!' one of her father's cronies shouted, before doing a last sweep of the room with his torch. Then they left, drifting out of the space and away.

Eve dropped her head to the strut in front of her. Burning tears threatened behind her eyelids, stinging the back of her nose as she held them in. She wouldn't cry, not now. Gage needed her to stay strong. There would be time to fall apart when they were together again.

'Boy, your grand-daddy was a liar and your daddy's a thief.' Her father again, cold and cruel. The tone all too familiar. 'Now you try to steal my *daughter*? If it's the last thing I do, I'll ruin you and your family. I will destroy everything you love.'

That voice sent icy dread freezing through her veins. She bit her lip to hold back a gasp. The metallic, salty tang of blood flooded her mouth. Hugo Chevalier would do exactly as he'd threatened. What had she done? She shouldn't have run. She should never have risked Gage or his family.

Someone spat, the sound full of disdain. She huddled closer to the beam but couldn't see anything. Her hands stung where the splinters had now worked beneath her skin.

A low laugh. Gage's. She trembled, wanting to scream out a warning. He didn't understand. Her father wasn't a man to taunt.

'You can't destroy everything I love, Chevalier, because you'll never have Eve. She's safe from you.'

A crunch like a fist on flesh turned her stomach to stone. She couldn't move, even though she was desperate to know Gage was okay. Shouts, noise. Cries of pain as he took a beating because of her. She should jump down, save him like he'd always tried to save her. He claimed she was one of the bravest people he knew, yet tonight she'd made him a liar, hiding like the coward she was.

She buried her face in the arm of Gage's coat, the earthy scent of the man she loved permeating the fabric. Reminding her of everything they were set to lose if things went wrong. There was no going back, not now. Eve sobbed into the damp fabric, the sound drowned out by the rain pounding on the roof above her.

CHAPTER ONE

Now

EVE SAT AT the expansive table in the plush boardroom with its million-dollar view over Seattle. Everything here screamed of a company on the top of its game with sparkling glass, gleaming wood, bright chrome. A company winning at everything, taking no prisoners. The last place on earth she wanted to be, yet a place she couldn't avoid.

She checked her watch. Ten past the hour. He was making them wait. She tapped her finger on the papers in front of her, stomach churning in a tumult of emotion she didn't think she'd ever untangle, no matter how many years she lived.

'I'm not sure this is a wise idea, Ms Chevalier.' She shot a stern glance at her lawyer, the man who'd served her family company for years. He was part of the problem and not the solution for what had gone catastrophically wrong. Yet she'd been forced to bring him, the board having trouble accepting her at the helm in lieu of her father. Trust was in short supply where she was concerned. She doubted she'd get any here either.

'It's our only option.' That was a truth that even the most pious believer in miracles could accept. The family company, Knight Enterprises, sat on the brink. Teetering, ready to plummet over the precipice into oblivion. If it died a swift and public death she'd survive. She'd been through worse than anyone could imagine—this was nothing.

Eve ignored the bright stab of pain that at any other time might threaten to crack her heart in two, the fleeting memory of a tiny white coffin in an empty church on a bright sunny day. There were far worse things than a company failing, but her mother and little sister had no chance if Knight folded. Protected to obsession, *controlled*, they'd fail right along with it. She wouldn't let that happen.

She'd done some things; terrible, hurtful things in her life. Destroying her mother and baby sister would never be one of them. *Never.*

'Your father would say otherwise. Your father—'

Another sharp glance sideways from her and the lawyer stopped talking. She'd become good at silencing people with a glance. Like father, like daughter. The burn of gall rose in her throat. Would Daddy be proud of her right now? She hated that he might be.

'My father is unconscious in hospital. He has no say here.' He'd been cut down in a way his enemies had never been able to accomplish. A mosquito bite, an overwhelming infection. It was hard to contemplate that something as mundane as an insect had felled the man now lying in an ICU bed in Jackson. She searched deep down for a shred of emotion, but all her energy was taken up with hiding the truth of her father's illness for now, while keeping Knight afloat.

Her father had forced them into this mess when he'd reset a ticking time bomb seven years earlier. She either defused it in this room or the whole thing blew up in their faces. Eve was an expert at defusing things. She'd done it her whole life. She'd do it again.

'Caron has been chewing at your father's heels

for years. You do this and it will be the end for Knight. Do you want that on your conscience?'

Caron Investments did more than chase after them. It was a behemoth, mouth agape, waiting to swallow them whole. A hatred between two families and business rivals had led her to this boardroom. She was currently reaping the toxic reward of all that loathing, but in her case that punishment was deserved. She'd fuelled the enmity, throwing petrol on a bonfire. In many ways, she was the reason they were sitting here.

Ultimately, one of the companies was destined to consume the other—she'd just never thought it would be Caron devouring Chevalier in its bloodied maw.

But today, it seemed, Caron would win the battle.

'If someone had told me what was going on, we may not have ended up here,' she hissed. She hadn't seen it coming, having been tucked away safely overseas. Hidden, inured from it all. She raised an eyebrow at the man sitting next to her, who now fidgeted with a pen and his compendium. 'But they didn't. And I still haven't received an explanation as to why I was never informed about the parlous state of things in the US. It's gross negligence on the board's part, which you should know, being the company lawyer.'

She reached for the glass of water in front of her, condensation slipping down the sides and pooling on a coaster protecting the mirror-like wood of the table. Gage was being rude with this lateness. A deliberate message.

'You're nothing. You have no importance to me. You are here at my bidding. Your fortunes survive or fail on my word alone.'

She could stand up. Go. Refuse to tolerate the slight and walk from here with her head held high and let everything implode around her. There was a certain wicked satisfaction in imagining that. Her father's one true love, his company, being destroyed at her whim.

But Gage had called *her* and requested the meeting. Well, not Gage himself but an assistant, requesting her attendance at his Seattle headquarters. That was enough to keep her in the chair, because she hadn't seen Gage in the flesh since that night seven years earlier. When he'd looked up at her in that gritty abandoned building, kissed his fingers and run, drawing her father and his men away from her.

The door cracked open and her heart rate spiked, a pounding that punched at her throat. Eve swallowed down the sickening sensation. She wouldn't allow anyone here to know her blood pressure pushed critical. She took a deep, steadying breath. Frosted herself over. Icy was a veneer she'd perfected years ago. No one could touch her, not anymore. She'd no tears left to shed. She'd cried them all as a naïve twenty-year-old. Her well was now truly dry.

Finally, he appeared, filling the doorway. Her breath was crushed in her chest, there was no air in the whole world enough to fill her lungs. All the years of seeing photos, reading about his business exploits on the internet, was not enough to prepare her for seeing Gage in the flesh again.

He strolled into the room, looking down at his phone, no acknowledgement of her presence at all. Not even that could hurt her, though, as she devoured the sight of him. His hair golden and perfect, every part of him the *golden boy* the press claimed him to be. He owned the room in a dark blue suit, crisp white shirt, red and blue tie. Bespoke, tailored to fit his impressive body. He loomed as a presence more than a mere man.

Like he owned everything around him—in perfect control.

Eve tried to keep breathing, tried not to show the effect he had on her because, damn, after all these years he still owned her body.

She hated him for it.

Gage grabbed the back of a chair while flicking through something on the phone screen. The leather dented under his grip. He pulled the chair out from the table. Undid the button on his suit jacket with calm precision and sat. Then—only then—did he look at her.

It was like being stabbed by an icicle. A cold thrust, deep into the heart of her, his vivid blue eyes piercing and frigid. Was he remembering the last time they'd spoken, in that terrible phone call her father had given her no option but to make? It was all she could do not to rise from this chair, say *Thank you for your time* and flee.

She'd never expected to have to face him again. She'd hidden out in France after being banished there seven years ago—the deal she'd struck to save Gage, to protect him from secrets he could never know. Secrets that would destroy him, and his family. She'd hold those in her heart for ever. Except she was done running. Running turned things into a disaster, as she and Gage both knew. They'd reaped the poisoned rewards of their own actions years before.

'Ms Chevalier.' His voice was all dark nights and silk sheets and her damned heart tripped over itself in guilty pleasure at the sound. 'Thank you for coming.'

Eve forced herself to look into his beautiful face. It was chiselled in a way it hadn't been in his early twenties. All softness had been hewn away, leaving a specimen of male near-perfection. The only thing marring it was the sliver of a scar under his right eye and the merest bump on the bridge of his nose where it had no doubt broken under the crack of a clenched fist. Her fingers itched to stroke over the flaws, to whisper how sorry she was for the wounds her father had left. But the cold disdain in his gaze told her there were no number of apologies she could offer that would make him forgive her.

'Gage. Thank you for inviting us here.' His eyes widened a fraction. She'd bet anything that everyone called him Mr Caron. Eve refused to play that game. While she might be prepared to beg for his help eventually, she'd start this negotiation as his equal.

'You can thank me at the end of the meeting when you see what I'm offering.'

'Getting straight to business. I like that.'

The corner of Gage's mouth kicked up in the hint of a smile that told her she'd pay, and he'd enjoy extracting the price. 'If you'd liked business a little more, perhaps Knight Enterprises wouldn't be in the desperate state that it is.'

Eve gritted her teeth. She'd tried to grab the reins when she'd sensed things were careening off track, but no one had wanted to listen to her. They'd parked her in France and let her play with the businesses there. The US was her daddy's domain, and he'd taken risks on things he shouldn't have. Too many chances that hadn't paid off. Now the company was fat and bloated and incapable of surviving the coming storm.

'My father and the board were responsible for the US division.'

'And yet you're here instead of him.'

Eve stiffened. She'd locked down news of her father's illness, determined to keep it quiet until she'd been able to assess the full scope of the disaster he'd wrought. The silence had bought her time, and that time had almost run out.

'Right where you want me?'

'I'd say almost the perfect position. Are you going to prostrate yourself? Beg me to help you wade your way out of the mire you've created?

Her solicitor started forward, beginning to rise from his chair. If he stepped in, she'd lose ground here. She wasn't some little girl who needed defending. She'd been fighting for herself and winning for years. Eve held up her hand and her solicitor stopped, sat back down, muttering under his breath. Gage raised an eyebrow but said nothing.

He'd soon learn she was no pushover, not anymore.

'The failings were my father's. His choices are not mine, and I refuse to own them for that reason.'

'I'm pleased to see you owning *your* decisions, Eve. Does that mean you'll take responsibility for what's coming your way?'

She reached for her glass, tried to keep the water inside still and steady as she sipped. The cold liquid hit her knotted stomach, which heaved in protest. She swallowed the sickening sensation down. She was made of stronger stuff now. She'd fought and won against bigger demons from her past than Gage Caron.

'I've never shirked responsibility for my actions, ever.'

He laughed, but there was nothing entertaining about the sound. Gage straightened some papers in front of him. Laid his perfect hands flat on the polished table-top. 'Well, hasn't this been fun. Let me be blunt. Knight's financial state is parlous. You've not grown organically or strategically but instead purchased anything and everything, particularly companies that Caron was considering.'

'If Caron considered them, I'd assume they were sound investments.'

Gage's eyes sparked something of a warning, a vicious kind of pleasure burning behind the polar blue.

'I rejected them as high risk with too little return.'

That's not what her father had said. Hugo Chevalier had taken delight in gloating, especially to her, about how he'd stolen yet another company from Gage, like some brutal, never-ending purgatory. Gage speared her with his frigid gaze again.

'Knight was welcome to them. Each and every one.'

Cold dread trickled through her. It wouldn't have been hard to manipulate her father, his quest for revenge all-encompassing, an unhealthy obsession. She'd only fuelled it by running with Gage, when all they'd hoped had been that the inevitability of a youthful marriage might heal the wounds between their families.

What a naïve, childish dream.

'Aren't you clever,' she said. Gage had planned this. Where once he'd been an avenging angel on her behalf, the sword he carried today would be used against her. He was revelling in their fall and part of her couldn't blame him for that. 'Let me share something with you. So am I.'

'If you're so clever, where are the investors? No one will touch you. The juggling act must be exhausting. Drop one ball and it's the beginning of the end. All it would take is a whisper in the wrong ear…'

The only piece of information held back right now was her father's incapacity. If that came out in an uncontrolled fashion, it was all over. She couldn't let that happen. Her mom and sister would never survive it. They were clueless about what was going on here, and that's how she wanted it to stay for now.

'It seems you know a great deal.' More than she'd expected. He was right, she'd tried everything, and doors kept closing in her face. It was as if someone had been chipping away, determined to make the Chevalier name meaningless. She was staring at the man responsible; she was sure of it.

'I've had seven years of solid study.'

'I like to think I can still surprise people.'

'There's nothing you can tell me about yourself I don't already know. It pays to have the measure of your enemies.'

A shiver ran through her.

Heaven hath no rage like love to hatred turned.

She'd bet anything that Gage didn't know everything, and she *knew* that she had some devastating surprises she could spring on him if she wanted revenge of her own. In some respects, she believed her father hoped that one day she would tell Gage all the secrets she held. But no matter how much vitriol he spilled on her, she wouldn't lower herself to joining the battle that had been waged by the two men so far.

'I understand what led us here. That's in the past.'

He picked up his sleek black and gold pen, twirling it nonchalantly in his fingers. 'If you don't learn from your mistakes, you're doomed. The past is instructive on what never to repeat.'

'Thank you for the lesson. Today is for looking forward.'

Gage smiled. Once that smile would have lit her up like a candle. Warm, genuine. Now there was no heat in it. It was a shark's smile, full of teeth and hinting of blood in the water and the bite to come. *That* smile chilled her to the marrow.

'Knight should be allowed to topple and fall. It's not a business. It's your father's vanity project.'

'Yet you called me.'

This wasn't an attempt at investment. It was a ritual humiliation. Revenge at its most acute from a man determined to destroy them all. If that was the ultimate end, Eve wanted to get it over with. She was tired of trying to prop things up when everyone around her seemed intent on cutting them down. If Madame Guillotine was bound to fall, she didn't have the energy to watch Gage sharpen the blade while she waited for it to slice her.

He steepled his fingers. 'There might be *some* aspects of the business that interest me.'

Eve let out a long, slow breath.

Let the games begin.

'What are you offering?'

'A lifeline.'

'I can feel the "but". What are the conditions? I'm assuming I won't like them.'

'Medicine isn't supposed to taste pleasant, Eve.'

'And I'm sure you're going to take pleasure in administering my first dose, so let's get started. I'm not big on procrastinating.'

'Your father will be removed as CEO.' Her lawyer spluttered. Funny, she'd forgotten he was even there. No matter. Since her father was currently in a hospital bed and she'd been carrying out the CEO's role in his absence, that was no problem. 'There will be a restructure. My word is *final* on what Knight keeps and discards. It needs to discard a great deal.'

'And will Knight retain its name and integrity as a company?'

'Caron will own eighty per cent.'

That was no answer at all.

Eve suspected there were many things Gage

had become, but a liar was not one of them. This wasn't a lifeline, it was a takeover. The members of her family held shares. Her mother and sister weren't interested in the business side of things, other than the money and security that it bought. If Gage took so much, there'd be nothing left and he'd squeeze them out. With their shares' current value, the offer on the table was almost worthless. She could rebuild. She had skills, determination and contacts outside her father's sphere. Her mom and Veronique wouldn't have a chance if she agreed to Gage's terms. She shook her head.

'Knight has a brand. The goodwill of the name is worth millions. You want that for some reason, so we come to this as equals.'

'How entertaining. There's nothing equal about us. You are so far below me in all respects, it should be considered a miracle I'm talking to you.'

She'd thought, "Better the devil you know", hoping that maybe Gage had wanted to see her, that things had mellowed over the years. That thinking had been a terrible mistake. She'd have to try elsewhere to find a saviour. A private equity firm perhaps, someone from overseas who hadn't heard the rumours. They might carve up the company but at least they'd treat her with respect to her face, even if they laughed behind her back.

'I will not sit here and be insulted, which seems to be the only reason you called me to your office. We have nothing more to say.' She stood. Her lawyer stood.

'Liar,' Gage murmured. Eve froze. Was she so easy to see through? Most other people couldn't read her, the frosty veneer she'd perfected years ago renowned. If she couldn't keep secrets from Gage, this would be a huge problem because her life was full of them. Gage leaned back in his chair, a smirk on his face. He turned to her lawyer. 'Mr Stoddart, I'd like to talk to your client alone.'

Eve nodded. She'd travelled halfway round the world to be here. May as well not waste the airfare before judging how this would play out to the end. Her lawyer looked at her with a raised eyebrow.

'I'll be outside the door if you need me. For the record, it has been a monumental error coming here.' He looked back at Gage as he reached the door and hesitated. 'You, sir, are no gentleman.'

'Ouch,' Gage said with a sneer as the board-room door slammed shut. He motioned towards her chair. '*Please* take a seat.'

'You're using your manners now?'

'I may as well, since I've just worked out how far I can push you before you walk.'

A fierce heat bubbled in her blood. He'd been playing her, and she'd fallen for it. She took a slow breath, trying to restore the equilibrium that seemed to have fled her. Lowered herself into the warm leather of her seat. Smoothed out her slim skirt, and there they sat in silence at either end of the long boardroom table. But no matter how large the room or expansive the wooden surface, the walls closed in on her. She took another sip of water. Tried to steer the con-versation back to some level of civility. It was the polite thing to do.

'I admire what you're achieving in Detroit. Repurposing those factories for renewable tech-nologies and retraining staff is admirable.'

'Flattery won't work here.'

'I'm not flattering you, it's the truth.'

He hesitated. Most people wouldn't have noticed. With Gage, she noticed everything.

'You been keeping an eye on me?'

She thought about the contents of a small, battered, yellow suitcase safely stowed in a hotel room in the heart of the city. A suitcase that travelled with her everywhere and held all her memories, physical proof that her eyes were always on Gage. She couldn't look away, even from France. But she'd never let him know it.

'I read the business pages like everyone else.'

'Giving unemployed people jobs and hope is the right thing to do. You believe in doing the right thing, don't you, *cher*?'

The pet name he'd once called her with so much love sounded bitter and poisonous on his tongue now. There were some memories she wouldn't allow to be tainted by all that had happened since, and this was one.

'It's Ms Chevalier, or Eve.'

Gage leaned back in the chair, the corners of his mouth kicking up for the briefest of moments. 'Eve, then. The original temptress.'

If that's what he believed, so be it. She deserved his rage, so she'd let him use it. As long as her mother and Veronique's fortunes were protected, she'd allow him to take his hurt and anger out on her. But Gage always liked a challenge, so she'd give him one.

'People only take the fruits offered them, if it's something they already crave,' she said, with a smile of her own. 'But enough of this. Why do I get the feeling you've asked me here only to mock me?'

'Allow me to indulge myself for a few moments. I enjoy watching you writhe under a good tongue lashing.'

His voice was low, soft. Overtly sexual. Heat roared to her cheeks and she was back on a picnic blanket, hidden under the cascading boughs of an old willow where he'd threaded flowers in her hair and indulged her naked body till she'd wept with pleasure. Gage smirked and the burning in her cheeks flamed hotter.

How dared he? He would not rekindle those memories, not now.

'That's childish and beneath you.'

He shrugged. 'I seem to recall you've levelled that accusation at me before. Or was it that you called me *common*? I'm not sure. Our final conversation seems to have been lost in the annals of my memory somewhere.'

It hadn't been in hers. She'd never forget each second of that last phone call, or the way it had cleaved her heart into a million pieces. With her father sitting next to her and Gage all but begging to see her again, she'd delivered the death blow to any chance they may have had of a reconciliation.

'It's over. You're being a child. This excess of emotion is common.'

She'd been cruel to be kind. Her father had promised that if she rejected Gage, he'd never reveal the secret he'd somehow discovered at a critical time for the Caron company: Gage wasn't the true heir to Caron Investments. He wasn't his father's child.

She'd refused to believe her father at first, until he'd produced evidence. A sworn statement from Gage's real father about an affair and the man's photo—it had been shocking to see how closely Gage resembled him. Then there were letters from Gage's mother about the pregnancy. Eve's father had been right when he'd threatened to find a way of destroying Gage's family. The information he had was the perfect bomb. It would have broken Gage to find out as he adored his parents.

She had refused to allow her father to destroy the illusion of his happy family, especially as Eve's own had seemed so bleak. Her father's obsession and quest for revenge. Her mother's illness, a woman always so frail and scared, preferring pills and liquor to her own children. Her sister's whole future hanging by a thread.

Gage's solid family was something he'd held onto like a shield. Promising that if she entered their fold, she'd be protected as well. She'd so wanted that solidity and love to surround her too, like a goose-down comforter. The realisation all those years ago that Caron had been struggling, and that news of Gage's parentage could tip the company and him over the edge, had devastated her. She'd do anything to save him from it. That's what true love was, protecting those you adored, even if it went against your own self-interest.

In her short life she'd become a master of it.

'Now that you've stopped watching me squirm, I propose Knight Enterprises keep its name. I'll take Caron's guidance on the less profitable aspects of the company and I'll support Caron purchasing a forty per cent stake.'

Gage's eyes darkened and then he laughed.

Part entertained, part jeering. 'You really think you have anything to bargain with?'

She shrugged. It was more vain hope than an expectation of reality, but she couldn't give up now. Because he'd come to her. Everyone wanted something. She just had to find out what Gage wanted from her.

'I'll give you points for audacity. I'm putting up the money and taking the risk for your poor decisions.'

'It's fixable and you know it. That is what you do, Gage. Break up what's worthless and re-build the good. If you were speaking the truth and this...' she waved between them '...is just business, then this is a good deal.'

'I'm taking the company. Seventy per cent. Knight is *mine*.'

'Fifty-five. My mother and sister's shares must remain unaffected. There's to be no detriment to their position. And they're to receive a parcel of shares each in Caron Investments.'

'A Chevalier owning shares in Caron?' he asked, his voice quiet and deadly.

She owned some. Privately. An investment through a trust so Gage would never find out she held part of him, for ever. It only seemed fair, since she'd come to realise he owned her, body and soul.

She'd shown her hand now, what she truly cared about. It was a risk, but if Gage understood one thing, it was the love of family. That's why she'd not allowed his own to be destroyed when her father had threatened it. 'You'll never let Caron fail. Their future will be assured.'

'What about yours?' Gage cocked his head, his eyes softened a fraction, and she saw the man she'd thought the boy might become one day, had fate and her father not intervened. He was breath-taking, and her heart ached for what might have been. But she cast the thought aside. No matter how Gage affected her, it would never have worked between them. Even ignoring the enmity between their families, they'd been too young to commit to a lifetime together.

'I can look after myself.'

She hadn't been able to once. But she'd grown up fast after being shipped off to France. At least she hadn't been locked up in a finishing school, which had been her father's first intention. Instead, she'd fought for a university education, negotiating with a ferocity she hadn't known she had while promising to make Gage suffer.

Her father had agreed. So long as a Caron was hurting, he was happy.

To protect Gage, she'd denied everything other than an infatuation. Denied Gage had touched her. Denied their love. Each one of those denials made her feel like Judas.

'I'm sure your trust fund makes life very comfortable.'

Let him think that was the only reason she'd gone back to her family, the money she'd been set to receive when she'd turned twenty-one. She didn't care. When her dreams of being with Gage had died, she'd used that blood money to fund another, her flower farm in Grasse. Her father had never understood her love of growing things, had refused to allow her to study horticulture, as she'd wanted to. It had been either a society wedding or joining the family business, nothing in between. So she'd chosen the family business and bought her dream for herself.

'It sure doesn't hurt.'

'It was all about the money, wasn't it?' Gage asked, eyes as hard as diamond chips. 'But I own you now.'

'Not yet you don't, since you haven't accepted my counter-offer.'

Gage sprawled back and the leather chair creaked as he did so. He turned to look out over the city that lay beneath them. Seemingly uncaring. A slight smile toyed on his perfect mouth.

'Sixty per cent. Your mother and sister can have their shares.'

Relief broke, washing over her. Not perfect, but she'd known she'd have to cede the majority of Knight to him. So long as her mother and sister's futures were assured, she was happy. She'd banked on him not destroying them too, and it seemed she'd been right. She released a long, slow breath. 'Thank—'

He held up his hand, stopping her. 'I'm not done. If you want this deal, I want something more.' He swivelled his chair round and stared her down. A ferocious businessman, burning with a vengeance. The shark had returned, circling. Even though the expansive boardroom table separated them, she wanted to get as far away as possible from the coming attack. She shivered and pressed back into her seat. He smiled again.

'Congratulations, *cher.* You're my new fiancée.'

CHAPTER TWO

THE COLOUR BLED from Eve's face till she was as white as the stark walls of his boardroom. It seemed surreal now that he'd had his hands all over that pale flesh once. A body now dutifully hidden under an impeccable, silver-grey suit that fitted her slender frame to a perfection. A fit that might make a lesser man weep with thanks. Not him. Not anymore.

He'd seen more of that skin than she'd probably care to remember, considering the way he'd seemed to disgust her only weeks after they'd parted. He'd stroked her in wonder, marvelling at the privilege of being permitted to touch her, to enter her lithe, luscious body. He couldn't shake that thought now, of stroking her responsive flesh till she moaned with pleasure.

He hated it. Hated that in the months after she'd finally rejected him, he'd tried to get over her. Had attempted to drown his sorrows in spirits and women who'd deserved far better than he had been offering. And still the memory of her had tainted everything. They'd been each other's first and some days it had felt like she was the only woman he'd ever truly enjoy, all others fading like a pale imitation beside the vivid memories of her. Like his body had recognised only one person as its own. Its other half. And without that there'd been a part of him missing.

He shook those thoughts aside. He didn't need them, not today. Not when he knew what she was. Flighty. Duplicitous. A consummate liar. She still hadn't responded to his pronouncement. Her plush pink mouth was opening, closing then opening again. Gaping like a fish caught on a hook and hauled from the water. For he *had* caught her and, by association, her father.

Bitter bile rose in his throat, but he swallowed it down with a grimace. All he'd needed to do was to choose the right lure and reel them in inch by inch. Just like fishing for bass with his dad. Easier, because Hugo Chevalier was nothing if not predictable. Anything he'd thought he could steal from a Caron he had, even if the deal was a dud. So long as Gage pretended to be interested, that was all Eve's father had needed. It had been surprisingly easy. Unlike this.

He hadn't expected Eve to put up so much of a fight. That she had stitched a thread of something like pleasure right through him. Another thing he'd be forced to ignore in time. And he had plenty of that. If she wanted to have some semblance of a company left at the end of all this, she'd do what he demanded. He relaxed back in his chair and waited. Made a show of checking his watch then looking back at her. He'd been waiting seven years so what were a few more minutes?

She seemed to compose herself. Gave a tremulous little laugh. 'You can't be serious.'

His simmering anger began to boil then. He'd done well to keep it under control so far. Playing this little game because he always knew the end point. Eve and her family had tried to smear his family's name since the night her father had hauled him off and given him the hiding of his life for having the *temerity* to steal away his precious daughter.

In the years that had followed, nasty whispers had abounded. Not enough to cross over into defamation, and nothing too public. Just a quiet word in the right ear whenever a deal was going to be struck or Caron Investments had achieved something great. That Eve hadn't been a willing party to their flight that rainy evening. That Gage was not a man to trust.

He'd be damned if that falsehood continued, especially now. It was time for Eve to pay. He'd make sure of it.

'I'm *deadly* serious.'

'Have you forgotten that in our great-grandparents' time it was frowned on for people who worked at Knight to even date a Caron employee and vice versa? The enmity has only become worse since then. This is insane.'

Yes. It was. But there was only one person who could quell the rumours that dogged him. The cause of them herself. She sat there stiff and straight, almost prim with her generous mouth pulled to a taut line. Not a part of her was anything other than perfect, right down to her sleek, tamed, golden hair. All the wildness smoothed and ironed out of her. He'd been witness to that wildness underneath. It was still there in the way her pale blue eyes flashed at him, making him crave for them to spark for reasons of pleasure, not anger.

He loathed how his body still reacted to her.

A siren's song calling for him to dash himself bloody on the rocks of their memories.

'It's the perfect narrative. I can see the headlines. "Fated childhood sweethearts together again, despite their warring families". A Romeo and Juliet story, without all the annoying death at the end. The press will eat it up.'

'We're not barely-out-of-our-teens runaways anymore.' She shook her head. 'No. It's not happening.'

How quickly she'd dismissed their past, but it would happen or she'd lose everything. She had nothing to bargain with here. He'd take Knight, carve it to tiny pieces. What he sought from her was more important than anything. Redemption, in the eyes of the business world and his family.

He would never forget the crunch of fist on bone or the cold cuffs crushing his wrists when he'd refused to tell Hugo Chevalier where Eve was. Then the disappointment on his father's face later that night when he'd come to the police station, bailed Gage out for the trumped-up charge levelled against him that had dissolved as soon as his father's lawyers had got their teeth into it.

All the approbation had been worth it...till Eve had resurfaced in the bosom of her family. The days he'd waited frantically for her call. Planning to go and meet her. Marry her and to hell with everyone. Until he'd realised he'd been fooled. That while she'd professed love, it had really been the thrill-seeking of a bored little princess who in the end had just wanted to dally with someone till she could get her hands on her trust fund. He gritted his teeth.

'I didn't make myself plain. That's the offer.'

'You can have seventy per cent, so long as my mother and sister's investments are protected.'

'No.'

He stood and strolled towards her. She pushed the chair out from behind the table as he neared, her hands gripping the arms.

'Eighty per cent.'

'You're part of the deal or there's no deal at all.' He towered over her now. She tilted her head back, eyes wide and pupils dark, her breathing fast and shallow. He shouldn't have enjoyed it as much as this, but he couldn't help himself. 'How long will it take before the creditors come to your door? Before your precious mother and sister are out on the streets? Till I own everything anyway?'

'If you're going to own everything anyhow, what do you possibly have to gain by this?' Her voice was rough and breathy. The throaty sound of it scored down his spine like he remembered her fingernails had.

He stilled. How dared she pretend? She was complicit in the suspicion that followed him. The women who'd chosen him, only wanting the bad boy. He was all too aware how a carefully placed whisper could bring everything crashing down. Sure, he'd done well. Working with his father, Caron had become a powerhouse, exceeding their wildest expectations. But Gage wanted more. Caron would be truly international. If he could secure the current deal he sought with the Germans—a deal he needed Eve's help to achieve, as much as it galled him—then the world would see what he was capable of. It's what he was owed, and Eve would pay up.

'I gain everything I want.'

'You want to marry me?' She blurted that out and he could tell she hadn't meant to say it. The mottle of red creeping up from her throat, marring her flawless skin, told him so. He laughed.

'Of course not. Don't worry, *cher*. It's only temporary and won't hurt a bit. Not unless you want it to. You know I always give a woman what she wants.'

The column of her slender throat convulsed. The thought of laying his hands on her flawless skin, had his body tight and on high alert. It was as if everything slowed, the air in the room becoming thick with possibilities. If he could touch her again, maybe she would be burned from his system once and for all.

'I don't want any of it.'

'Another lie, *cher*? How disappointing. You still want me. The whole of you tells me that like you're screaming it out loud.'

He could see it in the way her eyes tracked his every move. Surveying him, fixing on his hands, his mouth. Those parts of him he'd used to toy with her mercilessly the rare times they'd been able to sneak away from family and indulge their obsession with each other. And it *had* been an obsession. That's one thing she could never fake. The delicious heat of satisfaction slid through him.

'You'll agree. The engagement will last as long as it needs to, then I'll end it. And all the while you'll fake it with a smile on your face. History tells me you're good at doing that.'

She didn't even balk at the jibe, proving exactly what he'd accused her of being.

'And what if I want it to end?'

'That's not how this works.'

'I need to know.' She licked her lips, leaving them moist and kissable. Would her kiss still have the power to obliterate all rational thought? He craved to swoop down, capture those soft lips with his own. Loathed the fact that she still held some power over him. 'What's in it for you?'

'Apart from crushing your father by forcing him to believe that a Caron's hands are all over his daughter again, and that I've finally won? Let me see...'

He wanted to witness the look on the man's face when he realised he'd lost everything. His company. His beloved daughter. The world coming to know that the falsehoods he'd secretly whispered in the right ears had all been lies.

A look shifted across her face, fleeting, like clouds over the sun. 'There's something you need to know. Is everything that's said in this room absolutely confidential?'

'Don't you trust me, *cher*?' She winced at the endearment but he didn't care. Once she'd meant everything to him, and she'd thrown it in his face by trying to take him down. He'd never forgive her, ever.

'You're an intelligent man. This whole meeting was designed to take revenge against my family and we both know where that leads, to nowhere good. Of course I don't trust you.'

'The only person who has a problem with the truth, is you.'

'And yet here I am trying to tell you a truth and you don't seem interested.'

'I'm all ears.'

'I—I need to know that this deal is safe.'

'If you agree to my whole proposal until *I* say we're done, then yes. It's safe.'

The whole of her slumped a little. Her shoulders dropped. Her eyes shut briefly, dark lashes feathering over her cheeks. Then she opened her eyes, and that hint of vulnerability disappeared. Her eyes lost their soft baby-blue colour. Now they were all hard steel.

'My father's in hospital. The ICU.'

It was as though the earth shifted under his feet. The whole of him a morass of sensations that jumbled together in an uncomfortable soup of feelings he barely understood. There was disappointment that Hugo Chevalier wasn't going to see this, wouldn't feel the full weight of horror at the realisation that Gage had taken it all from him, but there was something else too, something that stuck like a knife under the ribs. A spike that felt a whole lot like sympathy.

He shook his head. He didn't have a sympathetic sentiment left in him. Eve had seen to that.

'How bad is it?'

She must be hurting. She loved her daddy. She had to, considering she'd chosen to go back to Hugo and her trust fund rather than keep running with him. Eve looked up at him, no expression on her face. 'He has an infection. They're worried about multi-organ failure. It's as bad as can be without being told to call a priest.'

She said it like she was asking him how he wanted his eggs for breakfast.

'I'm sorry.' The words stuck in his throat, but it was the right thing to do, to give his sympathy. He wasn't a complete savage—on most days, at least.

Eve didn't soften but appeared completely unmoved. 'No, you're not. But you needed to know because if it's revenge you're after, all you have is me.'

Her face was still impassive, as if it was merely business they'd been discussing. Hugo Chevalier's name had been the single thing holding that company together. One word about this spoken to the wrong person and Knight was done. He could have his revenge with no effort at all, but that would never satisfy him. He wanted the axe to fall by *his* hand. To know he'd won and taken everything for himself. So he still needed Eve, to achieve public redemption.

He hated it. Hated that he required her for this. Hated that all he'd ever wanted was her. Desire lashed him like a whip-crack as he watched Eve now. Her wide-set blue eyes, petite nose, luscious mouth, sleek hair. That beautiful body all trussed up in a business suit he wanted to snip at and unravel till she fell apart. It had always damned well been her, whether in love or revenge. She shifted in her seat and the gentle scent of jasmine and spring teased his nose, inflamed his blood. Made all of him hot and tight under the suit. He'd shrug off his jacket if he wasn't so damned hard she'd tell in an instant that while his head might loathe her, his body craved her with an unhealthy obsession.

'You'll do,' he said, his voice grinding out all rough and unrecognisable. She blinked fast, like something had been flung at her face.

'Was that meant to sting? Because nothing can hurt me anymore.' He wondered fleetingly what possible hurt she could have suffered in her privileged, protected life. 'It was such a long time ago, and we both know where revenge leads. It's beneath you.'

Sure, it might be beneath him, but while some memories in life had dimmed, one hadn't. Eve and those last weeks before the end haunted his dreams. Trying her phone in increasingly frantic efforts. Getting nothing then one day having her pick up. The relief that she was okay had flooded him, until she'd cruelly discarded him. From the tinny, hollow sound of the call he'd known he was on speaker and her father had been in the room, listening to it all. Doubtless gloating.

No, he could never forget.

He'd tried to exorcise her from his life. But to his fury every time he'd touched another woman, his body had rebelled. He'd cut a swathe through the female population at college, trying to drown out the memory of her, but he'd never been able to. Any time he'd seen the bright splash of golden hair or a flash of pearly skin his heart rate had spiked, thinking it might be her. But she'd been happily getting on with her life in France as he'd been trying to rebuild the pieces of his broken heart. It had taken years to forget the breathy sounds she made as she came. The smell of her, like the flower gardens she loved so much and wanted to create for herself. Time now to rid her from his life for good.

He sat on the table near her. Her gaze trailed down his shirt, hesitated on his tie, drifted to rest on the buckle of his belt and lower still. A swift shot of adrenaline punched right through him as her gaze lingered there a bit damn long. If she kept looking, she'd know exactly how much his cursed body still wanted her.

What if he kissed her? Would she react? By the flaring of her nostrils and her blown pupils he bet he could lay her out on this table and take her hard and fast till she screamed so loudly the lawyer outside would hear. Show her that, while he might not have been good enough to marry, she still wanted him.

That would be beneath him. Not this—an engagement as fake as the woman in front of him. If it could get the European deal over the line, it would be worth *everything*. Revenge was just a tasty morsel on the side. An *amuse-bouche*. Cleansing his palate for better things. It was time to get Eve out of his system once and for all. Because he'd never trust her, not again. She'd cured him of that gentler sentiment.

'That's easy for you to say, isn't it? You haven't suffered any consequences.'

Her brow creased. 'Consequences? I don't—'

'Enough. The innocent act, as compelling as it seems, doesn't suit you.' He stood, stalked to the other end of the table and grabbed a glass of water, taking a long, cold gulp. It didn't help cool the fire of anger burning in his gut. 'But don't worry. All it'll require is for you to pretend for a little while, which should be easy. I'm not trying to rekindle old flames and I don't want to tie myself to you permanently. Just long enough to get a deal over the line and then you're free.'

'A deal? Who is this merry charade for?'

He hesitated. She didn't need to know, there was nothing he had to tell her, and yet…she'd told him about her father. That was a devastating secret being kept from the business world, which he could have used to destroy everything without any effort on his part. She could have kept quiet about it till she had his money. He didn't understand why she had so willingly handed him the perfect means to ruin her.

Maybe it wouldn't hurt to tell her why he needed her. If she worked with him on this, rather than against him, their association could be over sooner. It's what he wanted, wasn't it? A tightness settled low inside him, like that thought was somehow wrong.

'Greta Bonitz.'

Eve's eyes widened. The German industrialist was renowned for her investments in renewable technology. Reclusive, private and family minded, it had taken one hint that Gage may not have had impeccable morals for her to cool and put their discussions on permanent hold.

With Eve as his fiancée, that would change. A partnership with the Bonitz group of companies would give Caron Investments what it should have had years before, premier billing on the world stage. He'd do that for his father, for all the times things had not gone as planned because of what Gage had done as a stupid twenty-three-year-old drunk on lust and a belief in true love.

He'd *finally* be relieved of this burden of guilt he'd carried.

'Why?'

'She needs to believe the lie that you and I are together. Help me get an agreement over the line and Caron will bail out your company and keep your precious mother and sister safe from the wolves already coming down the mountain for them.'

He saw the flare in her eyes, the intelligence ticking in a way that said she thought she might be able to find a way out of this. 'Take care, Eve. You've got more to lose than me. Fail, and I might lose a deal. You'll lose everything.'

'You're the only wolf at the door, Gage. You have been for years, haven't you?'

He smiled. She'd come to realise just how determined he'd been to bring them to this point, sitting across the table from one another with her future in his grip.

'Seven, to be precise.'

He saw the moment she knew she'd been backed into a corner she couldn't escape. She took a deep breath, straightened her spine and looked him in the face, her lips a tight, tense line. 'When do we start this fantasy?'

'You've got twenty-four hours to get things in order. We leave for Europe in forty-eight. I want to go through Knight's French holdings first. Then we meet with Frau Bonitz.'

'That—that's not long. How do I prepare my family?'

'I assume that's a rhetorical question. If it's not, tell them that after rigorously thrashing out our differences in the boardroom we concluded that we'd never stopped wanting one another. That should do it. Everyone loves a fairy-tale.'

Her cheeks flushed a gorgeous rose. Even though he loathed her, she was a beautiful woman. In her early twenties, he'd thought she was incomparable, but she'd been a pale imitation when compared to the woman who sat before him now. Fleshed out, with grown-up curves. It was all he could do not to reach out and haul her to him.

'We need the business side committed to an agreement.'

Business. Yes. He needed to remember. He opened the folder sitting on the table in front of him, scribbled relevant percentages in the blank spaces his legal team had already left on his instruction, and drafted a short paragraph allowing for the provision of Caron shares. That bit galled him, but it didn't matter. He would win far more than he lost in this deal.

He signed and dated the back page and slid it to Eve with a pen on top.

'Here's a memorandum of understanding. Our lawyers can sort out more formal details but this will do for now, since I never go back on my word. Unlike some.'

She picked up the papers and his pen slipped with a clatter onto the gleaming wood table-top. Then she read through the document slowly, her jaw clenched tightly. He fancied he could almost hear her teeth grinding. When he'd walked in today, he'd known almost exactly what he was prepared to offer, no more, no less. It was all about filling in a few blanks, which had cost him less than he thought. It told him how desperate she really was.

'Aren't you well prepared?' Eve ignored his pen like it was a snake sunning itself in front of her. Instead she slid an elegant silver fountain pen from her bag and signed in neat, precise script. 'How commendable.'

'I've had a long time to prepare for this day, *cher.*' Nothing took him off guard anymore. He allowed for every contingency. He'd never be surprised ever again. He'd waited long enough for today. He'd left nothing to chance.

'I thought after seven years you wouldn't care.'

He couldn't read what was going on behind her intelligent eyes, but she'd get a warning nonetheless that he wasn't one to be crossed.

'Oh, *cher.* Beware the fury of a patient man.'

Eve nestled into the plush leather seats of a jet sitting on the tarmac of a private airfield. She rubbed at her temple, trying to ease the throbbing that had taken up residence and didn't seem fit to move any time soon. It was as if her body had set out to spite her, ignoring the painkillers she'd downed as soon as she'd boarded. Even though her head pounded, she wasn't sure what hurt the most, that or her heart. It had been a close-run thing since Gage had burst back into her life.

She'd thought it would make things better, knowing the company and her mother and sister were at least safe from the worst that creditors could throw at them, but it hadn't made any difference, the dread replaced by another fear. Old doubts and regrets had resurfaced. The more she tried to shut them down the worse things became, so she allowed herself to sit with the thoughts for a short while. The 'what-ifs' she'd discarded years before.

They'd been too young. It would never have worked long term. These were the things she *knew*, that she'd told herself every day until the fantasy had died. Even if they'd survived the disclosures about his parentage and the ruination of his family, the seven-year itch would be settling in about now. It would be far worse for things to have ended up in a mess of recriminations at the hands of divorce lawyers than the way they had. A swift, clean break, no matter how painful at the time.

She just had to get through this, however long it took to play out. She could do it; she'd been through worse and while she allowed herself a few reminiscences right now, she wouldn't dwell on some memories. Not those of a tiny white coffin in a lonely church. Not of a baby born too soon.

No good ever came of memories like those.

Eve glanced over at the baggage cupboard where she'd stowed the little yellow case that travelled everywhere with her, which held all her grief and tears. She'd have preferred to keep it at her feet, but the flight attendant had reassured her with a smile that it would be safe. Maybe she could just go and check? She resisted the urge that welled up inside and bit at her heels. There had been days where all she'd done had been to sit and weep over the contents. Now, to simply know it was with her was enough.

Instead of needless worrying, she grabbed a magazine from a low table in front of her and flicked through it. Beautiful people, salacious gossip, fashion. It all blurred in a whirl of colour till she turned to an advertisement of a flower-filled field with a bottle of perfume overlaying the scene. A picture she recognised, the warmth of pride flowing through her.

That was *her* field. The farm she'd bought in

the south of France with the help of her trust fund and a loan from Knight's French arm. A breakout luxury perfume brand had bought *her* flowers to make their new flagship scent, and was keen to contract her exclusively. Especially since she'd hinted about the new rose she and her chief grower had developed. Her only regret was that she couldn't keep the property all to herself. Renting out the house for part of the year to fund her loan was a sad necessity. One day it would all be hers, but not for a while yet.

She smiled at this indulgence on the side her father didn't know about. He'd never understood her love of growing things. That was for gardeners—*staff*—and not his daughter. Getting dirty in the garden was something to be discouraged. Something beneath her. But it's how she'd first spied Gage. She'd been picking jonquils in the lower reaches of the garden and there he'd sat, staring down at her from the dizzying height of a huge old magnolia tree, framed by a sky as blue as his eyes.

That was another memory she shouldn't be wasting her time on. He wasn't that mischievous boy in the tree any longer. She wasn't that hopeful girl. They'd grown up, grown hard and moved on. Her focus was on building her farm. She could almost smell the scents of lavender, rose and jasmine hanging on the warm air and her headache eased a fraction. This was her happy place, where her worries seemed to leave her, the place she now felt most at home. She lingered a little longer on the picture as the flight attendant moved through the cabin and to the rear door of the aircraft.

'Mr Caron, it's a pleasure to see you. You're cutting it fine today.'

'Thank you, and my apologies to the captain and flight crew. Has my fiancée arrived?'

The ache inside intensified at the sound of his voice. She snapped her magazine shut and gripped it tightly in her lap.

'Yes, and may I offer my congratulations. Please take your seat and buckle up. If there's anything you need after we reach cruising altitude, just ask.'

Eve turned to see Gage coming on board. There should be a fanfare of trumpets heralding him. He was like some glorious corporate angel. Briefcase in hand, sporting a dark grey suit, pale grey shirt and silver tie, he stalked into the space with an authority that made her silly little heart swoon. He checked his phone before sliding it into his pocket and dropping into the seat opposite her. He was so tall his knees almost brushed hers. It was all she could do not to move away.

'Darling, it's good to see you,' he said, his gaze tracing over her body. She tugged at her shirt and wished she'd done up all the buttons rather than leave a few open, giving the merest hint of cleavage. At least she was dressed for business in a trouser suit. A reminder that for the foreseeable future every moment of her day was work. 'How did your family take the news of our engagement?'

The flight attendant walked back towards the cockpit with a warm smile for them both. Eve tried to return it, but felt sure what she gave in response looked more ill than pleased.

'As well as could be expected.'

Not well at all. She'd told her mom and sister that Gage had agreed to save the company. That they had unfinished business. Her mother had wailed about liars and cheats, betrayals and blood money, before taking to her room where she'd no doubt still be. Veronique had simply turned her back with the words 'It's treachery. He's a filthy Caron.' She'd ignored them both.

'What did your parents say?'

'My parents only want me to be happy,' he said. A tiny muscle in his jaw clenched, and she wondered about the truth of what he'd said. There was no warmth or caring in that voice. She could almost hear the sneer of *My family's better than yours.*

And as far as he knew, that was true. He was the only child, and doted on. Which was one of the reasons why the secret she held must always be kept. He'd idolised his father. Did Gus Caron even know Gage wasn't his? They'd always seemed to be such a small, happy family whenever he'd spoken of them. She wasn't sure her parents ever thought about her happiness. Not really. Her father was only interested in the dynasty, as if that warmed you on a cold night. Having two daughters had been a profound disappointment.

'I thought we could visit for Thanksgiving,' Gage said.

'That's...four months away. Will we still be playing this game then?'

'Since game-playing is your forte, it doesn't

matter how long this goes on. Sit back, relax and enjoy it.'

She blew out a slow breath and buckled up her seat belt as the captain announced take-off. 'Fooling people we don't know is one thing, but carrying on a charade in front of your family, in person? I can't and I won't.'

'You scared of being caught out as a fraud?' His eyes were on her, cold and hard like blue steel. He could hate her all he liked. She'd take his approbation, but he wouldn't push her around.

'No, but people get excited about weddings and you're their only child.' The lie almost stuck in her throat. 'I'm mindful of hurting the family you love.'

He looked out the window as the world raced by. Her stomach swooped as the wheels left the tarmac and the plane began to climb. She swallowed as her ears popped, and stared out the window too. Anything to ignore the man who sat like a force of nature in front of her. She could feel him, the air almost bristling and shimmering around him with restrained energy. It put her on edge, just when she needed to relax.

When he turned back to her, his face had

softened a little. Like the hard edges had been sanded away. 'No Thanksgiving, then.'

The plane levelled out and the captain announced they could release their seat belts, so Gage unbuckled his and strolled to the front of the aircraft into the cockpit. Eve couldn't help watching him go. His strong, broad shoulders, tapering into a narrow waist. The way his suit trousers sat low and firm on his lean hips. A prickly kind of heat rushed over her. She looked away before she ogled his backside because that had always been one of her favourite parts of him. The way she'd gripped him as he'd moved over her...

No. She would not go there. He'd grown up, that was all. Lost his youthful softness, his angles now hard and one hundred per cent adult male in his prime. Any female on the planet would be transfixed by all that golden hair, tanned skin and muscular physique, but obsessing about something she would never have wasn't worth the energy.

Eve sank back into her seat and closed her eyes, the painkillers she'd taken earlier finally taking the edge off her headache. She could work but nothing held her interest right now, everything depressingly bleak for the US operation. She didn't need to read the most recent reports emailed to her to know most of the businesses her father had purchased in the last few years hadn't lived up to the heady expectations of them. Or to know that the board's lack of due diligence was also to blame, believing her father when they should have been questioning the madness of his obsession with beating Caron Investments at all costs.

She might try to snatch a bit of sleep but as she tried to blank her mind and relax, the atmosphere changed again, like everything held its breath. She opened her eyes and looked up to find Gage standing in front of her. He reached into his coat pocket and removed something then sat in the seat opposite.

'This is yours.' He held out a small blue box. The knot in her belly tightened because she knew what it was and didn't want it. This was all a mockery, eating at her like a rat in corn. Still, she reached out to meet him halfway, trying not to touch him, not to let their fingers brush. She needn't have worried. Gage was as keen to avoid her as she him. He pulled back his hand as if any contact between them would singe. She looked at the exquisite, embossed leather ring box. It was still warm from the heat of Gage's body.

'It's unnecessary.' Why did her voice sound so faint? Once she'd been desperate to wear his ring. They'd talked about getting one after they'd crossed the border and married. There was no time beforehand and Gage had been devastated he couldn't do things the right way around—treat her like a princess, or so he'd said at the time. There was no point remembering any of that but, still, the difference between their dreams then and the reality now tore at her heart a little.

'You and I will soon be officially engaged. Of course it's necessary. Completes the blissful picture of our impending happy union.'

She could do this. It was only a piece of jewellery. It meant nothing.

And that was the whole problem, how meaningless this all was. It dirtied the memories of what they'd had together. Memories that had kept her going through seven years of long, cold, lonely nights. Memories of what love could be and what she might find for herself again one day.

No. There was no going back there. Her father had made it plain what would happen. Gage's family would be destroyed. Their business ruined. Gage would have hated her. Not immediately, but eventually. When the beautiful gloss wore off and everything was tarnished, he would regret the day he'd ever peeked over the back wall separating the two family's estates from his perch high in the magnolia tree, and said hello to a little girl picking flowers. That love of theirs would have morphed to hatred and they'd still be here, yet his life would be in tatters. She could never have done that to him. Love meant sacrifice. They were in the same place they would always have been. She'd done the right thing.

She had.

Eve lifted the lid of the box. Nestled in black velvet sat a huge emerald-cut sapphire, not dark but almost a cornflower-blue. The same colour blue as Gage's eyes. The magnificent stone was surrounded by baguette diamonds and framed in white gold. It glittered under the lights, precious and perfect. She breathed through the burn at the back of her nose. She'd dreamed

once of a ring like this when she'd been innocent, and everything had been simpler.

Her hands trembled as she lifted it from the
box. Slid it onto her ring finger. 'It fits perfectly.' The gem sat there, heavy and warm;
almost comforting, when there was nothing
comforting about this at all. 'How did you man-
age that?'

'I knew your ring size once.' Back then she'd
never expected anything like this. While their
families were wealthy, as two runaways they'd
had very little. 'I just sized it up a bit.'

She stilled. Stopped staring at the gorgeous
gemstone on her finger, as if trying to ascribe a
meaning to the sapphire it didn't have. Was he
saying what she thought he was trying to say?
She looked at him, narrowed her eyes.

'What do you mean by that, Gage?'

In all the time she knew him, she'd only seen
him embarrassed once. The first time had been
when they'd sneaked a kiss at the bottom of the
garden on her seventeenth birthday and he'd
tried to touch her breast. He looked a little like
that now. Eyes not quite holding her gaze. A
faint stain of colour on his cheekbones. It made
him look young, uncertain. Her heart ached for

that simpler time when everything had been perfect and new.

'It means I took into account that you'd be more...' He cleared his throat. She almost smiled at his discomfort. '...womanly now.'

He was right. Even though it had happened in her twenties, pregnancy did that to a woman's body. After she'd overcome the crippling grief of losing her child, losing every hope for her future, she'd relished the changes in her body the experience of pregnancy had wrought. The breasts that had never gone back to their normal size. Her wider hips. The curves she'd once have starved away in a quest for perfection, which she now wore like armour, always reminding her of the child who might have been. The little boy lost to her for ever. She refused to think about whether he'd have looked like Gage or like her.

She shut her eyes. Controlled the tears that she wouldn't let fall, not here. She coated herself in the icy indifference she'd perfected and opened her eyes again. Hiding from everyone what had happened to her. She looked Gage up and down to make a point but immediately regretted it. Being up close to him only accentuated how much he'd changed from a lean twenty-three-year-old to a vital man of thirty.

'Yes. We've all grown and sized up a bit.'

His nostrils flared. Gage looked down at the ring on her finger. A kind of heat burned in his eyes, which seemed even bluer than before. It slid through her like a jolt of spirits.

'Do you like it?' His voice was softer. He said it like he almost cared what she thought.

'I adore it,' she whispered, and he looked at her with the faintest of smiles teasing at the corner of his mouth. Vulnerability here was a mistake. She'd allowed herself that weakness once but now he'd wield it against her. She hardened her heart and her voice. 'It suits the narrative you're trying to fabricate perfectly.'

That banked heat in his eyes bled away till all that was left was a cold, unfathomable blue. Almost like he couldn't believe they'd had a civil conversation. He stood and she couldn't help but snatch a fleeting glimpse of the tight pull over the fly of his trousers, the unmistakeable bulge there. Heat rose from her throat to her face as he tugged his suit jacket closed and buttoned it, hiding the evidence of his arousal from view. The realisation that she might still affect him thrummed through her, potent and intoxicating. She could have moaned at the thought of it. How he tasted, how he smelled. Those memories didn't fade either, no matter how many times she tried to file them firmly in the annals of her past.

'It's a long flight. There's a bedroom down the back. You look tired. While it suits my narrative to have the world think I'm exhausting you with hours of lovemaking every night, you might not want the dark rings under your eyes for the inevitable pictures.'

She responded with a tight smile as he gave with one hand and took away with the other. She'd asked for it, and he'd delivered. Did he know how much he still affected her too? Did he care?

'I might just do that.' At least it would get her away from him, from this shimmering attraction that zapped through her. That made her crave things she couldn't have. Because that's what exhausted her every night. The lack of sleep, being woken by dreams of their bodies intertwined. His hands all over her skin. Exploring, probing. Those midnight fantasies were like an endless torment. 'Thank you for your concern.'

'I'm not concerned, *cher*,' he said as he turned and began to walk towards the cockpit again. 'I really don't give a damn about you at all.'

As she sat back in her seat, crushed under the emotional weight of the engagement ring on her finger, she realised they were both liars.

CHAPTER THREE

HE SHOULD HAVE allowed Eve to travel alone, but he'd wanted to test himself. To show that she didn't affect him anymore. That he didn't care. Yet those hours on the plane with her were a nightmare because his body cared, the clawing desire for her like an addiction that no drug could fix.

Even when she'd taken herself to the bedroom of the airplane it had ridden him hard—the need to open the door, slide onto the bed with her, see where it led. He'd lost control and had almost embarrassed himself after he'd given her that infernal engagement ring. Why the hell was he interested in what she thought of it? And yet the look on her face as her eyes had lit up, as she'd stared at the perfect gem on her finger... One of a kind. It had warmed something inside him.

He'd told her he didn't give a damn, and that was the truth. He didn't care, not even when he'd stood and she'd looked at him like her favourite kind of candy. None of that mattered. She was a means to an end. And then he'd end it. Redeem his family name, take Caron Investments and conquer the damned world. Move on with his life and finally be free of her.

To hell with his unruly hormones.

The car ride ahead of them now they'd landed was around an hour. But he was an adult and could survive at least that long. Gage grabbed his tablet from his briefcase and scrolled through some emails—tried to read a few financial reports—but his concentration kept wandering back to Eve with every elegant move she made, from checking her phone to reapplying her lip gloss or merely crossing her long, slender legs. His heart began racing in a thready, excited kind of rhythm like he'd been for a damned run without the benefits of taking any exercise.

Why hadn't he hired a helicopter to fly them the distance? But that would have been excessive. He understood his position of privilege in the world based on luck of birth and tried not to abuse it. Though right now he wished he wasn't trapped in this ever-shrinking space with her.

After not nearly enough time and yet far too much, she looked out the window and frowned.

'We should be there now. Aren't we going in the wrong direction?'

'And where should we be?'

'Nice.'

'That's where we're meeting Greta for dinner, but that's not where we're staying.'

He went back to work, numbers swimming as her scent filled his head. Something fresh and sweet and floral. Every time he saw damned flowers, smelled flowers, he thought of her. So he wouldn't have them in his offices or any of his homes, no matter how hard his staff tried to encourage him, because when he'd first spied Eve from his vantage point in the old magnolia tree she'd been clutching a handful of blooms and looking like the mythical fairy at the bottom of the garden.

He'd never forgotten that first glimpse of her, he would probably remember it till his dying day. How innocent life had seemed then...

'Earth to Gage. Some communication would be nice.' He realised he'd zoned out and gritted his teeth. Going mad as a result of this endeavour wasn't his plan, but much more time with Eve and he might totally lose his mind. He looked at her as she worried her lower lip. He wanted to slide his mouth over hers, ease the redness her perfect white teeth had left. Kiss her till they both forgot who they were.

Time to wrest back some control of this situation, let Eve know where she really stood in the hierarchy of things.

'My secretary no doubt advised you of our itinerary. Other than that, I'll inform you of anything I believe is important.'

'I see.' Her eyes narrowed, the watery blue of them darkened to something wilder, like the Gulf in a storm. 'You say jump and I ask how high. Is that how this is supposed to work?'

'You're getting the picture.'

'No, I'm not. You may be on your way to owning Knight, but I'm not some young thing you can push around. It doesn't mean you own *me*.'

The freeze of those words chilled his veins. He hadn't pushed her around when they'd been together. She'd wanted what he did, he was sure of it. But her words echoed every lie told about him. He couldn't let them go unanswered.

'What the hell are you trying to say?' That chill started cracking under the banked heat of his anger, always simmering just below the surface.

'I accept you'll never like me. You can hate me for all I care. But just because this ring is on my finger...' she waved her hand in front of his face '...it doesn't mean I have to accept you being any less than the gentleman your mother raised you to be.'

The desire to be a gentleman, to be a good man by any measure, had almost been wrung out of him years before. When he'd been beaten by her father and his henchmen, cuffed by the police, thrown in a cell, all for having the *temerity* to love the woman sitting in front of him. Wanting to *protect* her. He'd taken the beating, accepted the scars on his face and his soul for their love. Had kept his mouth shut as a *gentleman* who'd made promises would, and it meant nothing. 'And this assessment of proper conduct comes from who? You? Shouldn't a *lady* keep her promises, Eve?'

'It's a lady's prerogative to change her mind. Let's just say we owe each other nothing but civility. We're trying to pretend to have rekindled a great love. People will notice your barely concealed contempt of me. So let's start over. Gage, I'd like to know where we're going.'

Straight to hell was where he was headed.

Right now the colour ran high on her cheeks, making her vibrant, captivating. Incomparable in too many ways he refused to think about. He hated that he noticed this, how being round her made him feel more alive than he'd felt in years. As if he'd been in a torpor and all it took was Eve to awaken him. Because all he could think about now was how passionate she looked when she was angry, and how that flush on her cheeks reminded him of the colour that bloomed when she came.

But there was no room for those thoughts here, no matter how tempting they were, whispering seductively in his ear the things he'd like to do with her. France was all about work. The perfect start to his quest for redemption in the eyes of the world.

'Funny that you should ask, Eve. We're going to Grasse to stay at your flower farm. Since we're talking about rationalising the business, I thought it was good place to start.'

All that beautiful colour drained from her cheeks. He should have felt a spike of triumph, but instead he felt...*less*. Like a villain of some sort. But he steeled himself. It didn't matter. He'd been unjustly cast as some type of scoundrel for so many years he may as well wear the title with pride.

Eve didn't say anything. She dragged a tablet from the odd little yellow suitcase that she resolutely refused to relinquish even to his driver and which now sat at her feet. It looked like it had seen better days or a great deal of travel. He wondered at her keeping it when she was a woman who could afford a luxury brand. She was quite secretive about what it contained, manoeuvring the latch to make sure he couldn't see inside. In the brief glimpse he had, it looked like it was filled with old papers.

She tapped away with a kind of fury on the retrieved device, stabbing at the screen as she worked intently on something until they pulled into the property. As they drove through the gate and down the long gravel drive she looked up, out the window. Something on her face smoothed out. He hadn't realised that the merest of frowns had been marring her brow most of the time since he'd seen her again, until he looked at Eve now. A gentle smile tilted the corners of her mouth. A look of happiness, a quiet joy.

She used to look at him like that, once. As if

he were her safe place, her…home. Now he'd been replaced by this, a property, not a person. He didn't know what stung more.

The car pulled up in front of a quaint, two-storey French farm cottage of rustic stone overlooking fields of flowers. The pink of what he assumed were roses, the purple of lavender. He got out of the car and Eve followed, carrying her handbag and clutching the small suitcase tightly in her right hand. He reached into his pocket for the key handed to them by their driver at the beginning of the journey, but Eve was ahead of him with her own. She opened the front door and walked inside. It was a clear reminder to him that she believed this place to be hers.

'I trust this meets your approval,' Eve said, her voice clipped and sharp. She was dressed for business and he couldn't help admire the perfect fit of her deep blue pants as they moulded to her backside with every step. The cut of her jacket's waist that accentuated rather than detracted from her figure.

He followed the tap of her heels on the stone floor through a receiving room to the back of the house where French doors opened onto a patio, overlooking a lap pool and more flowers.

Sheer curtains billowed in the gentle breeze. The rooms were full of provincial French furniture, all wood and warmth. Paintings of flowers and landscapes adorned the walls.

The cottage was unlike any of the properties he owned, which were mere places he laid his head. They held about as much attachment to him as a hotel, kitted out by interior designers in cool greys, granite and chrome. This space, as exquisite as the décor was, looked like a home.

'It's beautiful,' he said. That was nothing less than the truth, when there'd been too little truth between them. 'You always wanted somewhere like this.'

Eve turned, put her bags on a table, its warm wood burnished by care and age.

'Don't forget. So did you.'

It was the type of home that they'd talked about owning together when their hopes and dreams had seemed to coalesce. But she hadn't wanted that future with him, and he'd been too blissfully ignorant being yanked around by the chain of his misplaced adoration to see it. It was a reminder. They didn't need each other. Once he'd thought that inconceivable but now he realised everything he'd done had been done in spite of her. He'd reached the pinnacle on his own.

She walked outside and leaned on the balustrade overlooking the sparkling water of the pool below and the beauty of the view beyond. In every direction were flowers, the scent of them lingering sublimely in the air. It all smelled like her—of gardens, of the life he'd expected to have. He stood back a little, not wanting to get too close. The warmth of the French afternoon sank into his skin and bones, unknotting him in ways he didn't want to contemplate. Everything here spoke of opportunities lost and fresh ones waiting to be plucked. He shrugged out of his jacket. Began unravelling in a way all too pleasurable to be safe, especially with her.

'You should have told me we were coming to Grasse,' she said, looking down at the azure water below her. 'I didn't bring anything to swim in.'

'I'm sure that doesn't matter here. It looks secluded enough.'

The words were out of his mouth before he could think. He imagined her in the glorious pool, naked, sliding through the water. Him right there with her, their bodies slipping against each other… Eve shot him a look over her shoulder, her cheeks tinged pink. She pushed herself off the railing and walked towards him, her lips slightly parted. Her pupils were big and dark in the pale blue of her eyes. It wouldn't take much to drop his head. Put his lips against hers. Kiss her like he had all those years ago. The need for it gripped him hard. This was a test as to whether he could finally overcome this craving for her. He hesitated then took a step back, rather than plunging his hands into the thick curls of her hair and dragging her against him.

'As tempting as all that sounds,' she said, stepping close and invading his personal space with a wicked tilt of her lips, 'I might just take a car to Nice and buy myself a bikini.'

She strolled through the doors into the house with her hips swaying in a kind of hypnotic rhythm and the thought of her in any of the boutiques, trying on their skimpy swimwear, filled his head with visions he was sure even a hundred laps in a cold pool wouldn't extinguish.

Eve adjusted the ties at the hips of the yellow and blue-two piece she'd found in Nice. She hadn't meant to purchase something so daring with its vibrant patches of fabric and alluring bows at the side, but she'd spent most of her life trying to stay safe and she was sick of it.

There was a fire in her blood that wouldn't be extinguished, not with Gage in *her* house, invading the space she'd once called her own. Fear gnawed at her stomach and she pressed her hand over the ache there. He'd brought her here for a reason and if revenge was that reason, he couldn't have designed a much better punishment than to take this place away from her. The one thing in her life she'd claimed for herself. She might not own it all, but she'd be damned if she would lose it without a pitched battle.

Eve checked herself in the mirror to make sure her stretch marks were mostly hidden. They'd never worried her before, the pale silvery lines being a reminder of what she could survive. She especially needed that reminder right now because a fight was coming. She couldn't hear Gage around so he was probably working on the press release for the announcement of their engagement, or planning some other kind of ordeal for her. One or the other, they were both the same right now, so to hell with it and with him.

She grabbed a floaty wrap that matched the

sun and sea tones of her swimwear and made her way to the pool. As she stepped out onto the patio she heard a splash. Eve looked over the balcony to see Gage's powerful form striking out in freestyle. Wearing tight black swimming trunks and gleaming bronze in the afternoon, the shimmering water sluiced from his back, his muscles rippling as he powered down the length of the pool, executed a perfect turn and powered back to the other end. Again and again. It was mesmerising, seeing him slice through the water, each stroke as hard and driven as the man himself.

It was all she could do not to sashay down there in her provocative bikini and slip into the pool with him. If this had been a grand affair, she would have. Would have stripped the little scraps of fabric from her body with a deft pull of a few ties and pressed herself into him. He'd probably reject her if she tried that now his level of disdain so strong it almost caused her physical pain to experience it.

No matter how strong the desire that flooded her with need, she wouldn't put herself in harm's way because of misplaced memories of a youthful love that they'd have outgrown had they stayed together. It was only because they'd parted that it had achieved such a mythic status in her own mind.

Anyhow, what did she know about seduction? Gage was her first and her only. She'd tried dating in the years after they'd broken up. Had tried to kiss another man but it had made her skin crawl. She'd resigned herself long ago to there being only one man her body wanted. Unlucky for her he was the wrong man. A man who hated her.

She turned her back on the tantalising view and instead found a spot in the shade on a sun lounge. Throwing on her sunglasses, she breathed in the warm, scented air and stared up at the flawless blue sky. The rhythmic splashing from the pool below lulled her. Whenever the world became too much, this was where she came. She'd never wanted to take over the family business. It had been her father's demand, drilled into her when the reality that he'd never have the son he wanted had hit home.

This, growing things, had always been her dream. To one day own the farm outright, move here and immerse her life in the soil and the scents of what she grew. Now it was possible that Gage had other ideas. That man did everything for a reason, and she wasn't sure of the reason why he'd elected to stay here in *her* home rather than in Nice proper.

As she ran through the possibilities, Gage appeared, towel lashed around his waist. His hair was rough dried and unruly. Drops of water sprinkled across his torso, sparkling in the sunlight like dew on petals in the morning. Dripping down his pectorals. Sliding over the ridges of his abdomen. Balmy heat bled over her, settling low and intoxicating. A delicious ache was building between her thighs. Her nipples tightened and she hoped evidence of her arousal was hidden by her wrap. He stopped when he saw her.

He made such an imposing picture, framed by the blue sky. His eyes a darker colour, boring into her. After the exercise his breathing was heavy, the muscles of his biceps and pectorals firm and defined. Would he look like that if he loomed over her now in bed? Naked, breathing heavily with passion and not exercise. A shiver of pleasure tripped through her and she tightened her wrap a little further, feeling weirdly exposed lying there, as if spread out for his pleasure alone.

And she had to say something, not just sit and stare like the fool she was, brain turned to mush by his hard, perfect body.

'Enjoy your swim?'

He ran his hands through his hair and droplets of water sprinkled the ground. 'Did some laps. I see you bought a bikini.'

His gaze drifted down her body to her bare legs, paused for a moment before coming back to her face. The heat of it was as sure as the caress of his fingers. A drop of water slid from the side of his nose to his lips. He licked it off. That, and the incendiary burn in his eyes, fired up the devil in her.

'I thought it was better than skinny dipping, since that wouldn't have been very businesslike of me, which is why we're here after all.'

'And yet neither of us is dressed for work right now.' Gage's voice was the rough burr of a sun-dried towel over her skin.

'I'm surprised you're not hard at it, drafting a press release on our engagement. I see the tasty morsel of gossip that you're off the marriage market hasn't hit the press yet.'

He cocked his head. 'Still keeping tabs on me?'

That wasn't far from the truth. For years she'd taunted herself with every alert about him. His success, failures—though there had been very few of those—the women...not as many as she thought she might see, but even one woman on his arm who wasn't her was too many. A constant reminder of what she'd lost, even though she'd convinced herself they wouldn't have lasted the distance.

No. Not lost. Given away because there had been no alternatives. She needed to remember there was a price she'd paid for loving him back then, and that was letting him go.

'It pays to know your enemies. And keep them close.' She crossed her legs and Gage watched the movement, his eyes darkening.

'So, now I'm your enemy, *cher*?' His voice was quiet, a mere whisper in the breeze. Their eyes locked. There was a heat in his, like a flash of sunshine on water.

'You tell me.'

'Perhaps you're not keeping me close enough.'

'Are we talking business or pleasure here?'

Silence between them stretched for a heartbeat. A moment in which hers fluttered in anticipation of his answer.

'Business, of course.'

Her shoulders slumped a fraction. No, she wasn't disappointed. Not at all. It was relief she felt. Blissful relief.

'No rest for the wicked, then,' she said. Except he didn't look wicked, he looked angelic, standing there half-naked, his hair drying in the warm breeze to the glorious blond gossip magazines raved about. Only soaring wings and a blazing halo could complete the picture.

Gage Caron. Golden Boy. Voted USA's most eligible bachelor three years running.

He smirked and she wanted to wipe that look of disdain from his beautiful face.

'No rest for you, at least.'

His words made her feel reckless when faced with all this potent masculinity. And she didn't care that they were enemies or that he loathed her. All she cared about was showing Gage that he might be a little affected by her, too. So she eased out of her reclined position, stood and took a few steps towards him.

'All work and no play makes Gage a dull boy.'

Another step and the pupils in his fathomless

eyes blew wide as she let the front of her wrap fall open. His gaze dropped to the slice of body it showed.

'You wanna play, *cher*?'

His voice was like midnight and sin and she desperately wanted to ignore caution and sell her soul to him, if only for the afternoon. Instead, she slid her wrap from her body. Tossed it behind her onto the chair she'd just left. She was close to him now and his eyes burned on her, his nostrils flaring, jaw clenched hard. Part of her was gratified she could still do this to him, that despite everything there wasn't indifference but an incendiary desire that threatened to consume them both.

It was her turn now to look him up and down. Long and slow. The bulge behind his towel was unmistakable. The power of that roared through her, making her feel as wicked as he accused her of being. If that's what he thought, that's what he'd get. She could almost feel herself sprouting horns and a tail.

Eve invaded his space, smiling as his fists clenched hard at his sides. She dropped her voice to as low and sexy as she could make it.

For a moment she held his gaze. His lips parted, like he needed extra air too.

'Oh, sugar,' she said, her voice dripping sweetness as she pointedly stared at the impressive evidence of the arousal there was no way he could hide, and drifted her fingers over the knot on his towel. 'I'm going for a swim. Looks like you'll have to play on your own.'

She revelled in the hitch of his breath as she brushed past and sauntered to the pool.

CHAPTER FOUR

GAGE FOUGHT TO overcome his desire for Eve, but he hadn't figured that being around her in person was *very* different from his distant memories. This morning he'd woken gripping himself hard after a night when his sleep had been plagued with images of her, his dreams and feverish desire bursting to life in full colour.

The feel of her as she'd brushed past him near the pool and his skin had become electric. The trace of her fingers over the knot of his towel that had caused his blood pressure to spike to near coronary levels. Now he was back to seven years ago when his need was fresh and the pain of unrequited adoration unbearable.

She was toying with him and he wouldn't let her get away with it. He'd recognized something when his mind had finally clicked back into gear yesterday. When he'd stopped salivating over her smooth skin on display in that magnificent bikini that had exposed much yet covered more. An item specifically designed to tease and tempt. Yes, once he'd stopped lusting after all that pale skin, elegant curves and her perfect breasts he'd noticed a few things as she'd stood so very close to him. The delicate flush of her cheeks, the way her nipples had pressed like hard knots against the fabric of her bikini top. Irrefutable signs she'd wanted him too.

What if he'd wrapped his arms round her waist, drawn her close? Plundered that pink, pouting mouth of hers. Laid her out on one of the sun lounges and buried himself inside her till she'd screamed his name.

She'd screamed his name long ago. He could get her to do it again.

Gage raked his hands through his hair. Took a long mouthful of hot coffee to try and jolt some sense into himself. Now was not the time or the place. He had to get his head on straight. Today they were talking Knight Enterprises and he'd been picking that company apart piece by rotten piece. There were aspects which were useful to him. As for the rest, it could go. Eve would soon learn that this was no game, and he wasn't to be played.

'Good morning.' Eve strolled into the room,

head high, a picture of confidence misplaced. She wandered over to the sideboard where a continental breakfast had been laid out, grabbed a large, white bread roll and poured herself a coffee.

Black. One sugar. He'd never forgotten.

She sat to the side of him. This morning she was dressed in elegant, slim-fitting black trousers and a crisp, white shirt, with her hair pulled back into a messy bun. She looked cool, businesslike, ready to do battle. Nothing like the pampered trust-fund princess he knew her to be. Her engagement ring glittered under the lights each time she moved her hand. Something hot, potent and possessive slid through him at the sight of it there.

Mine.

Absurd. Seven years ago he might have been desperate to see his ring on her finger. Not now.

'You don't have to wear it.' He nodded at the bright jewel. 'Not here, in the house.'

It did something to his equilibrium. Better she have it on only when necessary, which would be almost never, given that it was only for show.

She looked down at the twinkling gemstones. Splayed her fingers a little. Turned her hand so they caught the light. 'It feels safer here. I'd be scared to leave it somewhere, like the bedside drawer.'

Warmth kindled low in his gut. It felt good to watch her admiring it. When he'd seen it on a tray of jewels presented for his selection, it had immediately caught his eye and he'd only thought of her.

Yes. Mine.

That damned insistent voice. He ignored it. She wasn't his. She never had been and never would be. He wouldn't be fooled again, by anyone. He wasn't that young man anymore, full of hope for the future, desperately in love and made stupid by it. He'd *never* allow himself to be that man again and wouldn't waste more thought on what might have been.

'How was your swim yesterday?' he asked.

She took a sip of her dark coffee. Closed her eyes for a brief second in pleasure. Her lip gloss left a perfect pink stencil on the white porcelain and he wondered whether, if he kissed her, she'd taste like strawberries.

'Invigorating. How did you sleep last night?'

His blood rushed south as those dark, erotic dreams flickered in the back reaches of his consciousness. Not well at all. He'd ached for her the whole night. Lying naked in bed as he always did. The sheets torture against his overly sensitive skin. He'd never let her know.

'Perfectly. And you?'

'To be honest, I had a little difficulty. Until I…took things in hand. If you're ever having trouble sleeping, you should try it too.'

His mouth dried. Visions of her lying naked. Thinking of him. Touching herself and… He shut the heated thoughts down. Poured cold water on them. 'Try what?'

His voice sounded too rough and raw. He took another mouthful of coffee.

'Warm milk and honey, with a shot of bourbon.' Her lips turned up in a sneaky smile. 'Always works for me.'

She was playing him like a finely tuned instrument. No more. His desire for her was something he *would* control. He'd done it in the past. Having her here with him was the ultimate test and he'd win, get his deal done and move on. But how would it feel to turn the tables on her for once? Make her crave him like some addiction. Perhaps he could give her a small taste. He'd have her panting and begging and wanting him. He was older now. Wiser. More experienced than he'd been as a callow youth in his twenties. He knew how to push her buttons and push them he would, with immense satisfaction.

But that could come later. Pleasure would wait for now. He didn't want anything she didn't want to give. That was the triumph for him. Her desire. Her capitulation. Her *needing* him. It made the anticipation of what might come all the sweeter.

He finished his coffee, moved his breakfast plate aside. There were more important things at hand, for now at least. He was sure she wouldn't like what he had to say.

'We need to talk.'

'Ooh. Sounds serious.' Eve gave an exaggerated sigh. 'I suppose it's about business again. Remember what I said about you becoming dull.'

He opened his tablet and clicked on a file full of spreadsheets. 'About the French arm of Knight. I can email you—'

'I have all I need here.' She reached down, grabbed a tablet of her own and placed it on the table. 'But for this discussion I need some fortification.'

She buttered a fluffy white roll then slathered it in strawberry jam. Bit into it and slowly ate her mouthful while she swiped her finger over her screen, pulling up some documents as well. 'Go ahead.'

Her dismissiveness niggled at him like a stone in his shoe. He tried to ignore it. She was baiting him, and he wouldn't fall into that trap, not now.

'It's not doing as badly as the US business but there are a few areas of concern.'

Eve glared at him. 'We're doing far better than that and holding our own. Turning a profit.'

'You could do more.' He looked at the financials he had before him. He might have been more aggressive in his approach to some acquisitions, but the decisions that had been made had been sound, if not on the conservative side. 'The vineyard goes.'

She stared at him for a moment and he waited for the argument to come. Instead, she nodded. 'Fine. Next?'

That was too easy, and Gage was deeply suspicious of anything that came too easily to him. He expected more of a fight from her, on all things. 'You don't want to ask me why?'

A smirk played at the corners of her mouth.

'Why, sugar, you're my fiancé. I want to keep you happy. You should be pleased.'

He loathed it when she called him *sugar*. Gage narrowed his eyes. 'Are you treating any of this seriously?'

She narrowed her eyes right back at him. 'Deathly.'

'Then prove it.'

'You hold my life and my business in your hands and can do what you want.' Eve fiddled with the engagement ring on her finger. 'Will anything I say make a difference?'

'It might. I'm not an ogre.'

'I'll hold you to that the next time you behave like one.' She took another bite of her roll. Chewed deliberately. Washed it down with more coffee. 'The reasons for selling the vineyard are twofold. First is that it was my father's folly. You talked about vanity projects. This was one. Second, I'm betting Greta Bonitz wants a vineyard and that you want to sell Knight's to her.'

Gage sat back in his chair. What she thought about her father surprised him, because that's exactly what the vineyard was. As for the rest... 'Why do you think Greta Bonitz wants a vineyard?'

That little kernel of information shouldn't have been widely known. He had it because he'd been discussing it with Frau Bonitz before she'd turned cold on him.

'When you told me you were keen on doing business with her, I started researching. In an article a year ago she talked about honeymooning with her husband in Provence when they were young. Stomping the grapes at a winery. How it was such a fond memory. It got me thinking.' Eve finished off her breakfast. Drained her coffee.

'About?'

'How, given her husband's recent passing, she might want to hang onto those memories a little harder. Since she can't have him to share them with, maybe a vineyard in Provence might do.' Her voice was quiet and she stared out the French doors of the dining room to the view beyond. Still twisting the engagement ring like it irritated her.

As the silence stretched, he began to feel like there were things unspoken, subtext he couldn't translate. Eve got up from the table, walked to the coffee pot. Her long, lithe legs being encased in conservative black trousers in a strange way made her all the more tempting. A narrow waist he'd once loved to span with his hands. His pulse kicked up a notch. She turned and waggled her cup at him. He'd already had two cups this morning, which was probably the reason his heart rate was being unruly. Not the thoughts of how she felt in his arms, how he might try to get her back there. He shook his head as she poured another for herself.

'So, am I right?' she asked as she came back to the table with a full cup.

'Surprisingly, you are.'

She straightened in her chair, put down her cup and planted her hands flat on the table. 'There's no surprise about it at all. Do you have any idea what it was like, being a woman in her early twenties and given the responsibility of running a company without training?'

'You seem to have forgotten my involvement in Caron after college.'

'You had your father, who no doubt supported you. I had *nothing*. I might have topped my business degree at the Sorbonne, but I'd been thrown the French company as a punishment. Sent to a place I couldn't do much damage with every expectation I'd fail and be put in my place. I've had to work harder and be more prepared than anyone to get the board to listen to me. Even then it was a battle. Every day.'

Her breathing was hard, the colour high on her cheeks. A fight in her eyes, which were as hard and cold as blue diamonds. No society princess anywhere to be seen, and not the soft, sweet girl he'd known either. She was enthralling like this. He wanted to unpick all the complicated knots in her and see her unravel.

'I was *never* going to fail, and I didn't. So, Gage, what else have you got to throw at me? Because I'm ready for it.'

Her voice was as sharp as a prick of guilt. He looked at the long and mundane list on the computer of things that needed to change and back at her.

She ran her finger over a glob of jam on her plate, scooping it up and bringing it to her lips. His mouth dried. Memories assailed him of years ago. Of Eve on her knees in front of him. The biting pleasure even though neither of them had really known what they were doing. Well, he knew exactly what he was doing now. He'd have her on her knees soon enough. Perhaps he already did. That warm slide of pleasure through his veins was satisfaction. Nothing more.

'Here. The flower farm.'

She'd always loved growing things. Hanging around with the gardener, who'd indulged her. When they'd talked of the houses they'd own, her criteria had always been one surrounded by gardens, where the climate was right so she could grow roses. He'd planned to buy her fields of them when he could afford it. Instead she'd bought her own.

She stiffened. 'No. It's *mine*. Purchased with my own money.'

'Spent your trust fund, *cher*?'

'I could spend it in any way I saw fit and I did. On something just for me for once.'

As if he hadn't been enough, but history had shown him he hadn't been. It galled him that this was the symbol of her treachery. Well, she'd spent her money on what she'd wanted and now she'd have to deal with the consequences.

'It's not quite yours. There's a not so small matter of the loan Knight gave to support the purchase because you didn't have enough your-self. It's a liability the company doesn't need. Debts can be called in and this one should be because, like your father, you have a vanity project.'

'If you cared to ask, the farm is a business that's holding its own. You know it's making repayments to Knight on time, with interest. There's no vanity here. But this has nothing to do with how well it's doing or not.' Her hands clenched into tight fists on the tablecloth. Her lips a thin, taut line. Pale blue eyes burning like a gas flame. There was something enticing about her anger. He wanted to take it and channel it. Let it explode and consume them.

But he wouldn't fall into the trap that was Eve Chevalier.

Instead, he crossed his arms and settled back for the fight to come, the fight he'd been waiting for. 'What's it to do with, then?'

She stood and began pacing the room. Bristling with a tight and furious kind of energy. Her accent broadened then. Nothing like the smooth tones she'd obviously cultivated, those of a stateless world traveller. Hers was now a curious mix of Southern belle and French *ingénue*. The exotic sound of it raked down his spine as surely as her neat fingernails would.

'Revenge. Been there. Done that. Won't do it

again. You don't care how well the business is performing, you only care that it's important to me so you can punish me with it, which is petty.' She wheeled round and stopped, her eyes shining brightly as if there were tears there. Was she going to cry over this? Something sharp and painful stabbed in his chest. He rubbed at the spot. 'If there's anyone in this room like my father, it's you.'

'I'm *nothing* like your damned father.' He would not be compared to that man, ever. In response, she gave a sharp, bitter laugh.

'You've decided that because this place is mine, you're going to take it away. So tell me, how aren't you like my father? What is this, if not spite? Because, *sugar*, it sure isn't about business, since you know nothing about mine.'

He gritted his teeth, wanted to stand, face her and shout to the room that he was better than Hugo Chevalier. He'd proved it, in every way. Especially now, by winning. Except... Eve looked upset. The colour was high on her cheeks. Breathing hard. The tightness round her eyes that still sparkled too brightly. He didn't make a habit of upsetting women. He'd been taught better by both parents.

But more than that, if he broke through the anger, the emotion, there were things Eve said that didn't add up. Because she'd been given everything by her family. Money, security, running the French business. If there had been the expectation she wouldn't succeed, it had still been an opportunity some would almost kill for. Even then, she felt she'd lost...

'What did your daddy take away from you, Eve?'

Something flashed across her face as if she was stricken, and then melted away so fast he might have been mistaken. She walked to the French doors overlooking the flower fields and pulled the gauzy curtains aside as she stared at the view.

'That's not important anymore. This place is.' She worried at her lower lip with her teeth. 'I want to stop dwelling on the past and look forward. So, are you going to call in the debt? If so, I need time to re-finance.'

He heard the message loud and clear. He was the past, and that's the box she'd locked him into, but today there was still a niggle of something he couldn't put his finger on. Something he'd missed. Since Eve, he'd honed his observational abilities because he wasn't going to be blindsided by anything ever again. He'd get to the bottom of this, sooner rather than later.

'What if I was the bank? How would you sell it to *me*?' He didn't know why he was asking these things. Maybe he could indulge her, maybe he was going soft, maybe if the business stacked up...

'What did you say?'

She turned around slowly, like she didn't believe he could be reasonable and was waiting for the trick in his words. He didn't like that at all and didn't know why it mattered to him so much.

'Talk to me about your flowers.'

Even if this was the smallest of chances, she'd take it. She'd spent most of the night working on a proposal that she'd outlined in the car on the way from the airport the minute Gage had told her they were coming here. This was her one shot at saving what she'd fought so hard for. She strode to the table and turned her tablet to him. 'It's in here. Prove to me this is just business.'

He took the device and read. What she'd prepared was rougher than she'd like. There'd been little time to perfect it and too many emotions roiling around for it all to be cold, hard numbers and facts, but it would have to do. And still she had more, a snippet of information that she hoped would show Gage the possibilities. Excite him as much as it excited her.

He worked through what she'd done, scrolling through the document, his expression giving nothing away. She became transfixed by his hands. The way the veins stood out as an elegant cording under his skin. The strength she knew they held, cradling the device like it was something precious. His perfect fingers with their blunt, square nails shifting, moving back, forward. Sliding over her screen in the same gentle way he'd used to stroke her skin. Stopping…

He'd stopped. She swallowed down the knot tightening in her throat and sat at the table as Gage looked up. His eyes narrowed slightly, as if assessing her. The business was sound, the farmhouse rented most of the time, it was paying its way and its bills. These were things she knew a man like Gage would be looking for. Yet she couldn't get a read on his thoughts when he looked at her like he was trying to peer inside her.

'When did you prepare this?'

'Last night. I told you I couldn't sleep.'

Everything stopped at that moment. Even the birds outside seemed to have fallen silent, the breeze dropped. Like the world was holding its breath for her.

'Well done.'

The warmth of that small praise flooded over her, like the first brush of morning sun on her skin. No one had ever thanked her for her efforts or the job she did. Too many wanted to tear her down, whispering about how she'd been handed her position by her daddy, rather than earning it. No one knew the price she'd paid to be here, what she'd lost in the process. How much harder she'd had to work than anyone around her.

'But,' he went on, and she stilled. Her heart rate spiked. There was always a caveat, a 'but', a sting in every tail. 'There's more, isn't there? What aren't you telling me?'

Of all the things she'd read about Gage, there was one thing she should never have forgotten, that part of his skill in business was due to his freakish instinct. His ability to mine the secrets no one else could. He was right about there being more, but she could never let him have all of her secrets. She'd held them too close, for too long, until they'd become part of her. The burden she always carried.

'Why do you think there's more?'

'This document...' He motioned towards her tablet now lying on the table. 'It shows an excitement, a passion. Sure, the business is holding its own, but there's nothing here to be passionate about.'

Their eyes locked. A glorious heat settled in her belly then unthreaded and curled its way through her. The air seemed electric with possibilities, each one tempting but as unattainable as the other. Her passions had stopped being about a person long ago and had become about the little things accessible to her day to day. The smell of a rose, the cool breeze brushing sun-warmed skin, the sweet burst of a chunk of wild strawberry in this morning's jam. But now...

There was so much she could be passionate about here, if she allowed it. The hint of chest behind Gage's open-necked shirt, the strength of his tanned forearms sprinkled with golden hair, the pull of crisp cotton over muscular shoulders. All of that had inflamed her passions once, and it would be so easy for her to allow it to be so again. She eased her thoughts back to safer ground. Away from sliding her hands over those broad shoulders, pressing her lips to the pulse on his neck, letting him wrap his arms tightly around her...

Thoughts that would take her nowhere good. She ignored their allure.

'We've been trying to grow an enhanced rose. One with slightly different notes in the scent. Last year a bush showed promise so we cultivated a field of them and invited a few parfumiers here. Let their best noses smell it.' She paused, allowed the anticipation to build because there was joy in this, for her at least. Something she'd worked hard for and achieved on her own. And there was a tiny nugget of hope inside that people would be *proud* of her achievements. That Gage might be proud. A small thrill skittered through her at making him wait. Making him interested in what she had to say. Enticing him.

As the silence stretched, he raised an eyebrow and she relented. 'It started a bidding war for exclusive access. We're still in negotiations, but people are willing to pay a lot. It's—'

'Exciting' Gage finished the sentence, looking

at her over steepled fingers. 'And an achieve-
ment.'

What she'd dreamed of when her dreams of
having Gage had died.

Warmth coursed over her, heat rising to her
cheeks. She must look as pink as the roses in
her field right now. Here was a chance. It might
be tiny, but it was a chance nonetheless.

'What are you saying?' Her words might have
been a little too urgent, her voice a little too
breathy, but she didn't care.

The corner of his mouth quirked up in something of a smile, which looked a bit triumphant
for her liking, but if this was a lifeline, she was
taking it.

'I'm not bloody-minded about the process. If
a business stands up to scrutiny, it stays. The
farm does. For now.'

The whole of her unwound, as his words sank
in. Eve couldn't help the smile that broke out on
her face. In business she'd learned to hide her
emotions, but she didn't care about that now—
this was something to celebrate. She walked
over to where he sat, and he turned in his chair
to face her. He could still take her breath away
with those eyes of his, as perfect as a cloud-

less summer day. Her heart fluttered a few silly beats, as it always did when he was near. Around him she reacted like a girl barely out of her teens. He tilted his head back to look up at her.

'Thank you,' she said. All her tension seeped away, and something else entirely overtook it. A sensation so unfamiliar she'd almost forgotten what it meant. The surge in her pulse, the butterflies in her stomach. The bursting in her chest evidence of true happiness. She'd had so little of it in recent years. At that moment she didn't think too much about what she was doing as she leaned in and kissed him on the cheek, the merest brush. Something entirely platonic. Except the smell of him, all earth and spice, made her linger a bit longer than she should. Maybe she sighed. Maybe her breath brushed his cheek in a way it shouldn't have before she pulled away. She should move back to her seat, but she didn't.

'My pleasure,' he said. His voice was low and soft, better suited to dimmed lights and late nights than this morning in a breakfast room. And the sensations coursing inside her morphed into something else, something liquid, hot and potent. 'But that's not the type of kiss you'd give your fiancé.'

Her heart picked up its rhythm to something harder and faster. She should be terrified by this, but she wasn't. The anticipation of a coming dare overtook her. 'What do you mean?'

'We're having dinner with Greta Bonitz tonight. Our engagement won't be convincing to her if that's how you act.'

'I thought you were convinced I could fake it?'

'Time to prove it.' He held out his hand, palm up. His voice was a murmur, like a breeze through rose petals. 'Touch me.'

She should back away but his hand was there, and she craved to feel his skin against hers once more. He was right, in public they'd have to hold hands, at least try to look adoring, if this were to work. Maybe, just maybe they could reach some sort of truce here and now. She placed her hand gently in his. He wrapped his fingers round hers, stroking the backs of her knuckles with his thumb. All she wanted to do was close her eyes and give in to the sensation, his warmth, the gentleness of his touch.

'You scared, Eve?'

It was the game they'd played when they'd been kids and had sneaked off to the bottom of their respective gardens to see each other through the vine-covered hole in the wall. She'd always risen to the challenge of that taunt. Whether it had been climbing trees too high or catching garter snakes, a dare had always been her call to action.

She gazed into the everlasting and perfect blue of his eyes. She could drown in them they were so deep. 'You don't scare me, Gage Caron.'

His pupils were wide and dark, his nostrils flared. The knowledge that she still affected him jolted through her with the hot roar of power. He might be able to destroy her and her business, but she held something too. His desire. She wanted it, to wrest back some control of her own. Then he tugged at her hand. She followed with no resistance, allowing herself to be reeled in. Gage widened his legs so she stood between them, and drew her close with a smile that was all triumph. She swallowed, a pulse thrashing wildly in her throat.

'Who's afraid of the big, bad wolf now, *cher*?'

CHAPTER FIVE

SHE SHOULD RUN yet all Eve craved was to sink into Gage and take everything that his wicked smile promised. He was all dry heat and the crack and fire of an electrical storm, dangerous and thrilling. She was rooted to the spot, watching him blaze in front of her with a hypnotising energy.

This was a test of her determination. But if he thought the look of him sitting there as sinful as Lucifer would chase her away, he was sorely mistaken. She didn't run anymore. She never would again.

'Sugar, you'll learn that I'm no Little Red Riding Hood,' she said, her voice low and raw in a way that sounded alien to her ears.

'Who are you then?'

She cupped his cheek, traced the smooth, freshly shaven skin as she leaned down, her lips a whisper away from his. Breathing the same breath as if in that moment they shared one life together.

'I'm the woodcutter.'

Eve dropped her lips to his. She'd always marvelled at how soft his mouth was, but something about it caught her off balance today. That the hard man he'd become could have any gentleness left in him. This should stop, but she cupped his face and he slid a hand to her waist and gripped tight as he parted his lips and she followed.

Their tongues touched and she melted into the delicious taste of him, coffee and sweetness, and she could hardly breathe for the memory of it all. Those recollections flooded over her. Of their love, the adoration when everything had been perfect and unassailable. She slid her hands into his hair and gripped hard as he thrust his hands into hers, tugging at the pins that tamed her curls, scattering the infernal metal objects with a clatter on the table-top.

Their mouths clashed and warred and the kiss became a frantic thing with teeth and tongues and desperation. Gage hauled her onto his lap, never breaking contact. She twisted and then straddled him as he dragged her close till there was no space between them.

Years of dreams and desires collided in that one moment. She didn't care what it meant, what he thought of her. Gage had been her one and only. She couldn't contemplate another man touching her after he'd planted his seed during their one night of abandon, after she'd carried and lost their baby. It was too raw and too much and she just wanted to forget. Gage and his body could make her.

She couldn't stop as her hands roved over his shoulders and chest and relearned him, like a road travelled long ago. She worked his buttons with trembling fingers so she could stroke the hot, perfect skin beneath. Rocked on his hardness because he was right there with her, thrusting up as she moved, each movement causing a bright burst of pleasure to explode through her.

One hand released her hair, trailed down her body to her breast. His questing fingers stroked over her nipple. She groaned into his mouth so he plucked at it harder in the way she'd loved as she rode him. He remembered everything that drove her wild and repeated it, their bodies still in perfect tune with each other. Their breaths panted into the room as he grappled with the button of her trousers. Slid the zip down too slowly then eased his hand inside and stroked gently over her underwear.

'More,' she gasped against his lips, and the word was met with a low chuckle and fleeting pressure but not enough. She burned, wanted to tear off her clothes as they itched and prickled her skin. He eased his thumb beneath the waistband of her panties, sliding it with steady pressure over her slick clitoris. It took only moments for the burn to build and twist then explode outwards, her screams of pleasure trapped by their fused mouths. He kept going and the orgasm went on and on, wreaking destruction.

When she'd shuddered for the last time and sagged into him, limp and wrung out, Gage tightened his arms tight around her waist and stood. She barely had the wherewithal to wrap her legs round his waist as he placed her on the table in front of him. Her hands tangled in his hair; his mouth never left hers. Frantic hands grappled with the buttons of her shirt, tugged down the cups of her bra and he dropped his head to her nipple and sucked, torturing her till she writhed against him. She wanted him again, the exquisite emptiness building deep inside.

Gage somehow manhandled her pants down and off her legs. He pulled her forward so that she perched right on the edge of the table. The clink of a belt buckle and the burr of a zip told her they were far from finished and she didn't care. She never wanted this moment to end.

She reached out, craving to feel the heavy, warm silk of him in her hands, and then she took and gripped hard, marvelling at his glorious size and stroking him in the way she remembered he loved. He pulled back, moaned, mouth at her neck, kissing and nipping as a flood of heat built between her legs, aching to her core. He ran his teeth over and along the shell of her ear and the sounds they made were barely human, guttural expressions of need.

He tugged down the straps of her bra, pulled her shirt off her shoulders, trapping her arms, and she arched back, gloriously exposed. Gage's one hand slipped between her legs, fingers probing deep. The other tortured her nipple.

'I don't damn well care anymore,' Gage growled in her ear. It was like the words weren't meant for her, as if he was giving himself permission to take what he wanted. Then he kissed her again, all heat and battle, and she shook as though she was overwhelmed by a fever, with the impending orgasm hanging just out of reach. He pulled her closer or did she guide him? Then his fingers withdrew, leaving her empty and bereft till he notched himself at her entrance. She wrapped her legs around him again, encouraging, drawing him forward with her heels. He entered her with a sharp thrust and a groan. She tensed at the sensation, swift and over-full. It had been years and, no matter how wet she was or how much she wanted this, she couldn't help the gasp that escaped at the size of him. Gage stilled.

'Cher?'

It had never been Eve when he'd been inside her.

'A moment,' she whispered. She wanted his hands and his lips and possession, so she didn't have to think about him between her legs, invading her very soul. The short, shallow thrusts that had her panting and wanting even more. She raised her mouth to his, softer this time, gave a languid kiss that he mirrored as he slid in and out in a way she would have said was gentle and loving if it had been seven years earlier. The kindness of him at this moment would be her undoing. She drove her heels into the back of his thighs and tried to spur him on to something harder, less tender.

'Just...*take* me,' she said as she nipped at his collar bone.

'No.'

He slowed right down then, rocked into her, and she thought she'd go mad. He threaded his hand into her loose hair, wrapped its unruly length around his fist and eased her head back, her neck bared to him. Her breasts thrust forward, pushed up by the ruined cups of her bra. He licked and kissed and sucked and she was sure he'd leave marks everywhere as she groaned in frustration, bright light sparking in her eyes and the cliff of oblivion looming just out of reach.

All the while he kept up the rhythm, gentle and slow, and she despised him for it because what she wanted was hard and hateful, not this...undoing. Unpicking every seam she'd so tightly stitched up over the years. Only when he slid his hand between them again, stroked and teased and she began saying who knew what—unintelligible mutterings that were probably begging but she didn't give a damn about her pride—did he begin the hard thrusting that she'd craved, his rhythm breaking and irregular because he was as lost as her with the pressure and changes of angle.

In a roar of pleasure she fell apart, screaming his name, and he followed with a shout on one final hard thrust, filling her with his heat.

They stayed there for a few seconds, heavy breaths ragged in the room, the smell of salt and musk and sex hanging in the air, fused with the spicy scent that was all Gage. She closed her eyes, her head against his chest. The thump, thump, thump of his heartbeat in her ear. What had she done? His hate she could deal with. But a gentle, kind and passionate Gage Caron had the power to destroy her utterly and she wouldn't let him. She'd barely recovered the last time she'd let him go. She needed to move, protect herself from her own critical mistake. Allowing herself to touch him. Thinking the fire of their passion wouldn't burn her.

Eve raked up her bra straps. Shrugged her shirt back over her shoulders and pushed at Gage.

'Move.'

He slid out of her, still half-erect, hair a mess and looking confused as he stepped back, hands up and off her body. She ignored him and wrestled with her underwear, trousers. Anything to get away as fast as possible, to begin the process of putting herself back together.

'Eve?'

She shook her head as he tried to reach for her, tears stinging her eyes. Clutching her crushed clothes to her body as she pushed past him and ran to her room. She slammed the door and turned the key before stumbling to the bed and sitting on the edge.

Her body wasn't listening to what her head was trying to tell her, that this should never have happened. The unprotected sex, whilst blindingly stupid, wasn't going to lead to pregnancy. She had an implant so there was no risk of that.

No, it was that her body wanted more. More of Gage, his lips and his hands driving her out of her mind. Driving out the thoughts that whispered that if her father never recovered, some secrets would remain safe and she and Gage might one day have a chance, when there was none to be had at all. Not now or ever, because secrets had the power to destroy, and there were some secrets she would always have to keep.

What if he wanted more, too? She shivered, like she'd plunged into icy water. She craved that more than anything else in the whole world but there could never be any truth between them because she wouldn't destroy the family he loved. So they had nothing, because that lack of trust between them would rot everything away from the inside. Eve took a deep breath. She'd shore up her defences and inject the coldness into her blood that she'd become renowned for.

A sharp rap sounded at the door.

Time to be cruel to be kind. And the crueller the better.

No answer.

Gage did up his belt, having chased Eve to her room with his trousers half-open. Head still reeling at how out of hand one kiss had become. How much more he had wanted until Eve had fled down the hallway, half-dressed herself. He'd never hurt a woman during sex before, but she'd gasped and now he wasn't sure, not after she'd pushed him away and run, leaving him quite literally with his trousers around his damned ankles.

He had to get his head together, but sanity was somewhere back with their bodies locked in ecstasy at the dining table, with nothing on his mind other than the feel of being inside her again. The warm silk of her skin, the wet heat surrounding him. Eve's kisses, which had been desperate and wanting. The smell of her still clung to his skin, so heady and sweet it might never wash away.

It was as if he'd been transported back to a time where life had been perfect, a kind of surety that everything would work out. He hadn't felt that way for so long, the sensation shocked him. And Eve had been right there in the maelstrom of it all. So why run away at the end? Instead they should have both taken to the bedroom where he could have spent the day buried inside her, working her out of his system.

Gage tested the door. *Locked?* Hell. His heart began beating a sickeningly fast rhythm and he swallowed. All those rumours of him forcing her to go with him came back to the fore as bile rose in his throat. It was a moment's worth of insecurity that took him right back to her rejection. How he'd misread the situation totally. Had he done the same here today? He raked his hands through his hair. No. She'd been right there with him, screaming as they'd exploded together...

More... Just...take me.

She'd come twice and there had been *no* doubts in his mind she'd wanted him inside her, the passion overwhelming them both. Still, something was wrong, and he wasn't standing outside this room until he found out what it was. He knocked again, harder this time.

'Eve...' Damn, what was she doing? He felt like an utter fool, impotent with the inability to do anything other than ask for her attention yet again. He listened. Heard muffled sounds that he couldn't identify... Was she crying?

'Open up... Eve... Eve!'

He pounded on the door like a lovesick fool and hated himself even more for it, but he couldn't stop. Finally, the lock clicked and the door opened.

She'd changed her top to something black and body hugging. Tidied herself, with her hair now tamed and neat rather than spilling over her shoulders, perfect to grip. Presenting as cold and aloof as the day he'd called her, and she told him in no uncertain terms there was no *them* anymore.

'Stop that, sugar,' Eve drawled.

He hated that damned name. She only ever used it when she was trying to needle him and it worked the same now as it always had. But past that icy shell he could see the cracks that blurred and softened her. Mascara had smudged under her eyes, making them smoky. Her cheeks bloomed with a healthy, beautiful blush. Maybe not so icy and unaffected, then.

'We need to talk,' he said.

Her eyes widened a tiny fraction as a look passed through them. Something like fear. She swallowed, but her mouth held a tight, brutal line. Then she sighed theatrically and waved him away like an annoying child. 'I don't suffer from anything inconveniently contagious, and I'm on contraception. Unless you have something to add, there's nothing to discuss.'

Maybe he should have walked away. He didn't chase women, not anymore. He'd had a taste of humiliation at her hand once, and it was never happening to him again. And he would have walked had he not been certain he'd hurt her somehow. Asking the question was self-protection. He wasn't having any more rumours spread about him, not from her quarter at least.

'I'm clean too. There's no need to worry.' It was laughable how long it had been since he'd last had sex. He'd been so absorbed with his pursuit of Knight Enterprises he hadn't had time. Or that's what he'd told himself. The sad reality was that when he'd become focussed on Eve again, any other woman had ceased to exist. She'd become his sole obsession. The thought of touching anyone else left him cold, which had only added to his frustration and fuelled his desire to exact the retribution he'd sought for seven long years.

'We still need to talk. And I'm not having this discussion in the hall.'

He wasn't sure why it all seemed so hollow at this moment, but he wasn't letting the conversation go.

Eve stood back, held out an arm as if welcoming him in, but the hand holding the door gripped tightly enough he could see her fingers blanch white. He walked inside, looked around the space, focussed on the huge bed with soft cushions and creamy plush covers that loomed large in the room. How he wanted to carry her there and strip her cool façade layer by layer till she ignited again.

'It was *sex*, Gage.'

The way she'd said that word, spitting it out at him like they'd done something wrong.

There had been nothing wrong with what they'd done. On the contrary, it was the rightness of it that had shocked him the most. How natural it had felt, as if they'd never been apart.

'And if you need your ego appeased,' she added, 'an itch pleasantly scratched.'

'I'd say you found it more than pleasant. Since it took around two seconds of our kissing for me to have you on the table and coming, *twice*. That's reason enough for my ego to be doing fine.'

'It's been a while. And I didn't realise we were keeping score. Are you going to claim I owe you one now?'

He had been accused of many things in his time, but he *never* held expectations of a woman where sex was concerned. For him, giving pleasure was as heady as receiving it. While she owed him many things, the roil of anger began tightening in his gut at the suggestion she owed him that.

'Don't be ridiculous.'

She shrugged. 'Remember, I kissed you. And while it might have been my ass bare on the table, that one kiss proved I could have you right where I wanted you... Again.'

Her words hit him like a punch in the gut. At the time it had felt *all* mutual, but had she simply been using him, like last time? The burn inside turned molten, a furnace of rage that transported him back in time, welling and threatening to spill over. His jaw tightened hard enough to crack teeth. He'd let it damn well happen again and he loathed himself for it. He glared at her, standing there triumphant. So damned aloof. How could he have been fooled? She'd not always been cold like this. She'd once been a young woman full to the brim with emotion, or so he'd thought. Except...

He took a breath through that surge of fury and as he did so realised that she wouldn't look him in the eyes right now. If she didn't care, she'd be looking at him straight on and not somewhere in the middle of his chest where she seemed to have developed a fixation with his shirt buttons. So instead of listening to what she said, he focussed on how she'd acted instead.

The flush over her skin, her pleas for more, *harder*. Leaning against his chest, accepting his arms around her as they'd taken a moment and come down from the cataclysm that had been the intimacy between them. Screaming out his name and then pushing him away hard and running like the devil himself was chasing her. Locking the door. He hesitated.

She's scared.

Of him...

No. It wasn't him. It was something else and he'd find out what it was if it killed him. He could taunt her like he'd always done as a child, when something had terrified her. She never backed off from a dare but now he began to suspect her lashing out with claws unsheathed was something else. Her trying to force his distance. Right now he enjoyed her claws a little too much because they were both spoiling for a fight. He could give it to her, because making up could be a thrill all of its own. Except he didn't want to fight with her, but *for* her, and he knew the ways he could play dirty and win.

What had always had her melting like but-

ter on a summer's day had not been playing
rough—though they'd done their fair share of
that and it had been fun—it had been the gentle,
tender moments. So she was angling for a fight
right now. He wouldn't give it to her because it
was easy to fight when he bit at the hook she
cast for him, the one that fed the anger he carried. He'd just have to play smarter, not harder.

'I'm sorry I didn't think about contraception.
It was irresponsible and wrong. If you don't
trust me, I can get tested again, for your peace
of mind.'

Her eyes widened a fraction.

'No, I trust you.' Her whole body softened,
wilted like something had come loose. Like he
might be winning this game, with the rules he
didn't understand. Then it was as if she'd reminded herself she wasn't allowed to be vulnerable anymore, and everything in her hardened
again. 'But you are a man after all. Led around
by one thing. It's always the same.'

He took the barb, absorbed the sharp stab of
it. Ignored the twist of possessiveness like razor
wire wrapping round him, at the thought of any
other man with her. He had no rights here, none

at all. But being around her flung him into a kind of insanity that made him a fool.

'Cutting me down to size?'

She held her head high and proud. 'It was easy to do. You're soft wood.'

He laughed, because now he *knew* she was lying. She dangled that damn bait so enticingly, but he wouldn't take it.

'Yet only minutes ago you were ecstatic with how hard I was. I wasn't hearing your complaints, only your screams.'

Eve glanced at the bed, at him, then back at the bed. Took a small step away from it like if he was too close to her, she'd tumble him onto the mattress. He was enthusiastic about that idea. It was right where he wanted her, eventually. There he'd get more truth than any conversation they were having right now. Something was going on here and he'd find out what it was sooner or later.

'Eve. Enough of this. Let's agree you're an expert at hurting me. Thing is, I'm worried I might have hurt you.' He'd lowered his voice, tried for something more conciliatory. 'I'm sorry about that too.'

She turned away towards the windows, reached

to her face and swiped her fingers across her cheeks. Was she crying? He took a step forward, wanting nothing more than to reach for her. Her tears had always broken him, and that sensation of needing to comfort was an overwhelming thing that had his fingers itching to take her into his arms and soothe away whatever pained her.

She gave a sharp, shaky kind of laugh. Wrapped her arms round herself as if holding something in. 'I... It didn't hurt. As I said, it's been a while.'

It would have to have been a hell of a long while for it to surprise her, hurt her, or whatever she'd experienced. He had no rights to her. She was an adult woman who'd left him long ago, but masochist that he was, he needed to know or it would niggle like a splinter under his skin.

'How long?'

'Long enough.' She shook her head, looked at him with her pale and haunted eyes. 'Not that it's any of your business.'

Eve looked at her bed again, yet with so much yearning this time it almost cut him off at the knees. A pulse began beating, seductive and low, that primal drive he knew too well, one that he accepted now that he'd probably always have around her. He was half-hard again, and she'd be able to see that. Earlier he might not have wanted to give her that power over him, but he didn't care anymore.

'I could guess.'

'And in the unlikely event you were right, would you expect a prize?'

A slow smile slid across his face. 'I'm thinking a better idea is something where we both win.' Part of him was secretly pleased he still knew the ways to make her come apart at the seams.

'I refuse to play these childish games. It's a mistake to mix business with pleasure and, anyhow, I can get pleasure anywhere.'

'You can't get it while you wear my ring on your finger. Anyhow, you don't want it anywhere, you want it from me.'

She tugged the gleaming sapphire from her hand. He gritted his teeth as she walked to a feminine-looking dressing table and gently placed it on the pale wood.

'Every man thinks they're special. You're not. Please leave, I have things to do.'

He needed to go. She wasn't giving up her quest for an argument, and he still wasn't in control enough not to risk uttering hurtful things that couldn't be unsaid. In his darker moments when he'd thought back to that night she'd cast him aside, he'd imagined her gloating at the pain she'd caused. She didn't look like she was gloating now. Her face was pale, her eyes tight as she chewed on her lower lip. At this moment Eve did not look like a woman who enjoyed hurting him. She looked like the young woman he'd thought he'd known and had believed he'd spend his whole life with. One who'd been kind, protective of her mom and sister. Loving.

'Then I'll leave you to wrestle with your feelings for me,' he said, and walked from the room. What had happened to her between the time he'd left with only their kisses under the sound of the rain as memories, and the day she'd ended it all?

Hugo Chevalier had happened, and Gage was determined to find out what that man had done. There were any number of ways he could go about getting that information but she'd tell him in the end because he had a weapon she couldn't fight.

She still wanted him.

CHAPTER SIX

EVE SNATCHED UP her evening bag and headed for the door of her room then stopped, looking around. There was a needling sensation, like her world was not quite right. Like she'd forgotten something. She turned and her gaze lingered on the dressing-table, where her engagement ring glittered in the low lights.

She looked down at her left hand and the sense that something was missing increased. Eve turned back, tossing her clutch onto the bed as she passed. Grabbing the ring, she slid the extravagant cluster of gemstones onto her finger. They lay cool against her skin, easing the burn of her overheated flesh.

Eve tried not to think about how comforting the weight of the engagement ring was whenever she wore it. She hadn't realised properly how any of this would be, having believed she could cope with her feelings. Sadly, she'd underestimated how crushing unrequited desire could really be. How the cruel words she'd forced herself to say would chip away at her soul and blacken it for ever.

It had been one thing as a desperate, besotted twenty-year-old. When her father had found her in that rundown hotel, she'd been fuelled by fear and exhaustion, and in the horrible weeks that had followed she'd agreed to anything to protect Gage, her choices horrible yet clear. She'd also had the advantage of not seeing him. That distance had made the terrible choices seem easier. No one had witnessed her weeping into her pillow every night.

Soon she'd been a continent away from him after their last, terrible call when she'd destroyed his love for her and succeeded in turning it into blind hatred. But nothing had prepared her for the wearying exhaustion of the act she continued to play.

Eve smoothed her hands over her blue dress, perfect for travel because it was soft and body-hugging and had once made her feel beautiful. It also now made her feel exposed, the fabric the same vibrant colour as Gage's eyes, matching her engagement ring to perfection. It clung to her body and reminded her with each movement she made of Gage's hands softly stroking her.

She tried to ignore that sensation as she walked from her room down the stairs to travel to dinner with Greta Bonitz, blinking back the threatening tears. Kissing Gage, touching him. Making love, because it had been far more than sex. They had all been a critical error. Once their lips had touched it had been like her body had come home. The soul-deep sigh of relief.

But now she was left with lonely nights in a bed in a house where he lay just down the hall, because as much as her body wanted him again and again, she couldn't let him have her. That realisation crippled her. If she let him touch her again, she might never let him go, and where would that leave them?

He wanted her, that was clear. They still burned brightly when they were together. While she had nothing to compare it with, their bodies didn't lie like their minds did. They knew how to work together in perfect synchronicity. She shivered. Closed her eyes and let herself indulge in the guilty pleasure of recalling the feel of him inside her again. A flood of warmth washed over her.

And now she was simply avoiding him. She took a deep breath to steel herself and walked down the hall to the lounge. Gage waited there, staring out the doors that showcased the view of her fields of flowers. Night had fallen now and everything was in darkness, but the breeze still blew in perfumes of roses and lavender. He had his hands in his pockets, coat slung over the arms of a chair. His shoulders were broad and strong. Once they'd carried so many of her burdens. Now she only had herself. She let herself indulge in the look of him, surveying the darkness outside as though overseeing his domain.

'The car will be here soon.'

She didn't know how he knew she was there but, then, she'd always known when he'd walked into a room so perhaps he had the same sixth sense about her too. It comforted her and distressed her all the same, with the what-ifs. What if she'd ignored her father's threats? What if she'd still run back to Gage? Would they still be together? Would their baby...?

No. There was no use to these thoughts. She'd punished herself enough for the last one. She didn't need any more.

He was such a beautiful, masculine picture

framed in the doorway, glowing in the low lights of the room. The golden boy indeed. Gage turned and raised a tumbler a quarter full of golden liquid.

'Drink?'

Not unless it was straight bourbon. That might be the only thing that would get her through this. But she needed her wits about her, especially tonight when everything felt so ragged and raw. 'No, I prefer not to drink before an important business deal. The celebration can come afterwards.'

'Looking forward to getting rid of me that quickly?'

The smirk on his face told her exactly what he thought she might say, and exactly what her answer really would be if she told the truth. And that was a worry in and of itself.

'You know we both want to move on, sugar.'

The corners of his beautiful mouth curled in a sensual smile.

'So certain of that, are you?'

His voice was as gentle as the warm breeze floating into the room, but it packed the power of a punch. Did he want her, still? The slide of his gaze over her body gave her the answer, but she wouldn't admit it.

'I'm certain of what I want.'

'Hmm.' He didn't press further, merely sipped his own drink, the ice clinking in the glass, and watched her. Blue eyes were supposed to be cold, icy, but his burned hot and ignited her. If she didn't know it was impossible, she might worry about self-combusting right here in the middle of the room.

'You look beautiful,' he said, and strolled towards her, moving in close. He placed his half-finished drink on a side table then reached out his hand and hesitated. She didn't move away, and he seemed to take that as a kind of permission. He gently grasped one of her blonde curls between his fingers. 'I love your hair like this.'

His voice had a kind of wistful, contemplative tone to it. She couldn't deal with that. His anger, his dislike—they were easy things to accept. Not this quiet man, the one who reminded her of the twenty-three-year-old she'd run away with.

'Thank you,' she murmured, and didn't think too hard about how she'd left it down on purpose. Gage looked magnificent himself, standing there in a blue striped shirt, open at the neck and showing a tantalising slice of chest. The narrow taper of his waist. The way the trousers framed his strong thighs. Thighs she'd wrapped her legs round only hours ago. Heat rose to her face. An ache bloomed deep inside her.

'I like the look of my ring on your finger.'

That doused her heat like falling into a pond in winter. The problem was she liked the *feel* of it on her finger. She loved the sensation that it was his claim of ownership over her. Something about that thought slid way too much warmth and pleasure through her blood, like a good shot of spirits. She'd never wanted to believe anyone owned her, but Gage had. He'd claimed her heart and she hadn't been able to entrust it to anyone else. Damn him. She looked down at the exquisite gems with as much disdain as she could muster, which was hard when the ring was the most beautiful thing she'd ever seen.

'Your ring might be on my finger, but you don't own me. You never did and you never will.'

'I owned you this afternoon for a little while.' He held up two fingers and his smile was all devil. 'Twice, if I recall.'

'You're not being a gentleman about this.'

'I learned my lesson well. You taught me there was little point.'

'I'd rather forget about this afternoon.' If she didn't, she'd just throw herself into his arms and beg him to tear the clothes from her body. They might never make dinner.

'Whereas I'd like to do it again. Many, many times.'

She stopped breathing. No air would come. The atmosphere was too syrupy and thick. She wanted it again too. Craved it. Would do almost anything to be in his arms again. All she had to do was to walk forward. Kiss him… But no. That would end in disaster.

'You're deluded.' Her voice sounded more like a breathy whisper of desire than a denial.

'I'm a realist. Sex was never the problem between us. We're adults. Why not enjoy ourselves?'

Because he'd move on and she'd be wrecked for ever. Except the temptation of it rang loudly. To forget everything but the feel of his lips and hands on her body. Him inside her. To be lost and found all rolled into one. She tugged at the tie around her waist, loosening it a fraction. Everything seemed too tight. Her skin was fit to burst with wanting.

'I promise we'd enjoy ourselves. It would only be better the next time. And the next.' Heat radiated from his body. The smell of him, all bespoke cologne and something else. The essence of the man himself. Earthy, raw. She wanted to lean in, rest her head on his hard chest. Give in to this thing between them. It was all she could do not to slide into his arms again and tuck herself in where she felt safe, one of the only places she did. But he wasn't safe. He was her greatest danger and she'd be a fool to ever forget it.

Still she looked up at him, into his fathomless blue eyes. She couldn't tell what was ticking away in that clever brain of his. They were so close now and in her heels she could tilt her head up and kiss him. Allow herself to forget for a little while…

But forgetting was dangerous. She'd tried over the past seven years and hadn't been able to. The contents of her small yellow suitcase were testament to her obsession and her grief. Then the sound of an alert interrupted the moment and Gage broke his gaze from hers. He checked his phone and she stepped away from him, taking a deep breath to regain her equilibrium.

'The car's here,' he said, and began walking to the door as if their conversation about sex had never happened. And perhaps for him it didn't matter. She was a means to an end. A vehicle for his revenge against her father. To her, it was like her world had tilted on its axis. She was sure people could be grown up about this. That adults could sleep together and not care. Just have fun. Scratch an itch. She wasn't one of them. She'd never be casual about Gage Caron.

Letting him touch her in the first place had been a mistake.

The night air was warm as they slid into the back of the car, a driver holding the door open for them. She steeled herself for the journey to the restaurant. Tonight was important, playing her part even more so. Success here meant her freedom sooner. Once Gage's business with Greta Bonitz was confirmed, their engagement would end and she could melt into obscurity. Retire to her flower farm, grow roses and forget Gage Caron existed. But the thought of handing back the engagement ring and trying to pretend she and Gage had never touched, never kissed filled her with torment. Better to remind herself that this was a business arrangement.

'How close are you to finalising something with the Bonitz companies?'

'We've stalled.' His voice was tight with the sound of repressed anger as the car began the journey to Nice. 'Greta is an extremely family-minded woman. Her own marriage lasted forty-seven years before her husband passed away and left her at the helm of the Bonitz group. It's important for her to work with like-minded people. I caused her some...concern.'

She didn't ask why and he didn't seem keen to offer more, simply staring out the window and shutting her down. She did the same for the rest of the drive. Tried to forget that Gage was so close, that she could simply reach out, touch him if she wanted. Take his hand.

None of that was clever or wise, yet she didn't feel either of those things right now.

The car slid to a halt outside a restaurant. Her heart began to race with a sickening rhythm. Her mouth dried. She wasn't sure she could do this. There'd been no need to pretend when they'd been alone. Here it was another thing entirely. Her mother and sister's futures hinged on the success of tonight. In many ways, hers did too.

'Don't you think she'll wonder about the convenience of you suddenly producing me?'

'No.'

Gage didn't wait for the driver but opened the car door himself and hopped out. Eve followed. He held out his hand to her and she looked at it for a few seconds.

'Hold my hand, Eve.'

She slid hers into his. The warmth of him engulfed her, but she was rooted to the spot. Rather than drag her into the restaurant behind him, Gage drew her close. Took his free hand and cupped her cheek.

'Do you want to know why she's not going to question a thing?'

Eve couldn't speak. She shook her head, wanting to melt into the warmth of his touch. Absorb the strength he exuded.

'This,' he murmured.

Gage dropped his head to hers. Their lips brushed. And her mind blanked.

Kissing Eve was like heaven and hell. Something he craved. Something he'd give almost anything to do again and again. When his lips touched hers the shock of it jolted through him. He forgot that they were standing in a street in front of a restaurant. He forgot everything but the feel of her soft lips on his own. How she opened underneath him and gave to the kiss as much as he took. This might be one of the most important nights of his career, but he didn't care. He wanted to call the car back and take her home. Peel off the soft dress that clung to her curves. Take her to bed. Bury himself inside her for hours. Hell, they mightn't even make it home the way he felt. Even the back of the limo sounded good right now. Dark. Private. Anything to be alone.

A click. The burst of a flash. Gage came to his senses and broke the kiss. He turned and there stood a man with a camera.

'The cameras,' she said, her voice husky and low. Her cheeks flushed a glorious pink. Eyes glazed, pupils blown wide. A tendril of satisfaction curled through him that he could make her look like this. Drugged with desire. 'Are they—?'

'Here for us. Yes. The news of our "engagement" dropped today. Our romance will be all over the gossip sites in no time and that kiss is why Greta won't doubt a thing.'

Eve seemed to come back to herself, the blush on her cheeks intensifying.

'If that's all it takes, I could have been any-one.'

He gritted his teeth. She still wasn't taking responsibility for how she'd got here. For the rumours that he'd plucked her from the loving bosom of her family, and she'd been *afraid* of him. Morphing their past into something twisted and dirty.

'You know why it had to be you.'

A slight frown marred her brow. A look of confusion if he hadn't known better, but those rumours had to have come from somewhere and she'd never tried to scotch them.

'I don't—'

'We should go inside.' He refused to hear excuses, how she was not completely aware of what she'd done, how she'd not been party to the rumours that had surfaced time and again. Whenever he'd felt like he was getting some purchase, another ugly whisper had started. That he was a man not to be trusted. 'We don't want to keep Greta waiting.'

He led Eve into the restaurant, and was ushered to the table he'd booked in a softly lit and private corner. Greta was already there, waiting. An elegant older woman and a powerhouse of the European business landscape. She stood as they came to the table. No smile, which didn't bode well, but at least she'd agreed to meet him. It wasn't something she accorded many people. He smiled instead, held out his hand and they shook.

'Frau Bonitz.'

She waved him away. 'Please. You make me sound ancient. It's Greta.'

'Thank you,' he said. 'And this is—'

'Eve Chevalier.' Greta cocked her head, her brown eyes intelligent and intent. 'I know all about you. I've been watching your activities in France with interest. Your efforts at building the European side of Knight Enterprises are impressive.'

Gage glanced at Eve. She smiled, and this one was wide and genuine. 'That's an accolade, coming from you.'

'I'm always alert to young women on the rise in business, because their efforts are missed by most.' Greta turned to Gage. 'But not you, it seems.'

He shook his head. 'I've had my eyes on her for years.'

Eve's hand jumped in his. He squeezed it gently. She seemed to relax as they sat at the table and he ordered champagne. Discussed choices with the sommelier, all the while listening to Greta and Eve talk.

'Knight's portfolio is an interesting one.'

'Yet we're looking to reorganise and sell a few companies that don't quite fit into our current strategy. Gage and I are in France, trying to decide which ones. Our vineyard is likely to be the first to go.'

'Hmm.' Greta took a sip of water as the waiter poured their champagne. 'We may need to talk some more about that.'

Eve cleverly guided the discussion, but she clearly already had Greta on the hook for the vineyard. Her skills in drawing out the conversation about a possible sale were subtle and impressive. So subtly done that it didn't affect the mood of the evening at all. He might be wrong, but it seemed Greta had warmed to him by a few degrees, and that was all Eve's doing.

Greta picked up her glass of champagne. 'I understand congratulations are owed to you both.'

Eve smiled and looked down at her ring, which sparkled under the low lights. Something about her seemed wistful and a little sad. 'Thank you. They are.'

They toasted, glasses clinking round the table. 'And yet your families' rivalry is renowned. I hope for your sakes they took it well.'

'Mine were circumspect,' Gage said. The lie niggled uncomfortably. He'd travelled to see his parents to give them the news, not wanting to tell them in a phone call or, worse, for them to find out through the media. While he'd told Eve they just wanted him to be happy, his mom and dad had not reacted well.

'Still, Gage? Didn't you learn last time? We told you a Chevalier can never be trusted. Ever.'

His mom and dad wanted a wedding, grand-children, but that would never happen with Eve. Right now he couldn't see it happening at all. Would his parents be happy when he ended things? Likely. Gage took another a swig of his champagne, a waste of a magnificent vintage because he was unable to savour it. None of this felt like triumph to him. It all seemed hollow and pointless.

Eve toyed with a napkin on the table-top. She huffed out a laugh. 'Mine will take a lot of convincing.'

The honesty and pain of the answer surprised him. Without thinking, he reached out his hand, placed it on hers and squeezed. Eve's skin lay soft and cool under his own. She gave him a watery smile and a moment passed between them, something he couldn't explain but which felt a lot like understanding.

'I'm sorry. Family is important and my life's greatest reward,' Greta said. 'To work with my children, I can think of nothing more fulfilling, and I hope that for you. Although usually the gossip magazines have tales of burgeoning romances like yours, there's been no hint of anything between you, which is a surprise given your reported history.'

Gage stiffened. Pictures of him in his twenties being hauled out of a police car with a bruised and bloodied face had been excellent fodder for the gutter press. Gage's greatest shame was the suspicion he'd brought on his family in those times. He had said nothing to reporters, maintaining a dignified silence. But those pictures were easy for anyone to find, if they looked. Even though he employed people to ensure his online reputation was clean, there were some things you couldn't hide, no matter how much money you paid.

Gage let Eve's hand go and was about to reach for his glass when a discreet waiter leaned in to refill it. If Greta had any suspicions about the truth of their engagement, a check of the internet tomorrow would have photographs of their kiss and that would quell any uneasiness.

'You don't look like a person who'd read gossip magazines.'

'Usually I don't, but I'm interested since I'm a romantic at heart. Given the past, what started your reconciliation?' She turned to Eve. 'Since you've spent the past seven years in France, it would have been difficult for you both to cross paths.'

Eve leaned forward like she was going to tell a secret.

'Few people know this but Knight's having some liquidity trouble in the States. Gage offered to invest,' she said smoothly, placing her hand on his arm. Gazing at him with her head to one side, her pupils big and dark. 'He rode in like a knight in shining armour to save the day.'

Gage laughed, that recollection absurd but sounding so real. 'I think, *cher*, that description owes more to fantasy than reality. I seem to remember I was more corporate raider than white knight.'

She laughed too, something in her eyes flaring as she did. 'Maybe you were a bit piratical. Somewhat of a marauder.' Her lips curved into a sultry smile. 'I obviously like that about you. That's the power of our love. It's never changed.'

The words tore through him like an electric current. A waiter handed them their menus, but for him the words blurred on the page. They'd said they'd loved each other so many times in the past. He'd believed they had but had come to learn love wasn't for him, it hadn't been for years. He'd lived first-hand through the pain of betrayal and couldn't do it again, although on some nights, late, the thoughts crept in. What if they'd stayed together all those year ago? Could they have had a relationship as long as Greta's?

He'd never know. Gage quashed the thoughts, ignored the ache inside. Of overwhelming loss, of missed opportunities. He was made of harder stuff than this. And he didn't care anymore. This was all a means to an end.

They ordered their meals. Ate the exquisite food, which he barely tasted as he watched Greta and Eve talk because any involvement by him proved unnecessary.

Eve was perfection—warm, engaging, genuine. There was no flighty socialite at this table, no precious society princess. She and Greta connected as if they were old friends. He was mere garnish on the side.

And even though it was all going to plan, his anger began to simmer and boil. He breathed through it. Sipped more wine. Sat back and laughed on cue, commented where necessary, but couldn't completely hold back the burn. This could have been them for real. Yet Eve had thrown it all away, and for what? Daddy, Mommy, a trust fund? A damned flower farm in the South of France? He would have bought her the world if she'd asked for it. They could have done it all together, not spent these years apart.

But Eve *couldn't* have loved him. Love wasn't cruel, like she'd been. Love was about protecting the person you adored. No matter how good the sex still was between them, no matter that there appeared more to their story than he'd assumed over the years, she'd still strung him along and dumped him when convenient. Once this was done he'd do the same and walk away without a backward glance. He *had* to.

The twisting in his guts only hinted at the lies he told himself.

'This has been a most engaging evening,' Greta said, bringing him back into the conversation.

Gage smiled. 'I hope there can be more.'

'I'm holding a soirée in Munich in a few months' time. I'll send an invitation to you and your lovely fiancée.'

Gage glanced at Eve but didn't wait for her affirmation. 'It would be our pleasure.'

Or a descent into hell if they couldn't burn through this consuming attraction between them. But none of that mattered right now. He'd do almost anything to get this deal across the line. Eve didn't look happy with Greta's suggestion. The too-wide smile that didn't reach her tight eyes was a giveaway, to him at least. Good, this wasn't about her entertainment but about paying him back for the *years* he'd spent trying to undo his youthful foolishness.

Though why did it feel all so petty?

'Your approach to me was interesting,' Greta went on. 'I don't work with just anybody and I am gratified to see the rumours aren't true.'

'What rumours?' Eve asked. Gage tensed, all of him on high alert. She might not have spread them herself, but she would sure as hell have known what her daddy was whispering about him.

'You know, *cher.*' He turned to her. He'd look her in the face when he confronted her. The whole charade they were playing was about this. Redeeming his image so he could take his rightful place at every table without snide whispers. 'The story that says you didn't want to elope with me. That you weren't a willing participant.'

'That's ridiculous.' The words were adamant but all colour drained from her face. She gripped her napkin tightly in her hands. So tightly her knuckles paled.

'Of course it is,' Greta said. 'People saw a romantic story and took joy in making something unpleasant of it. *Schadenfreude.* But I can see it isn't true. I only wish you as long and as happy a marriage as my husband and I had.'

Eve turned to Greta, gave her a tight smile.

'Thank you. We can only hope to be as lucky.' She dropped her napkin on the table and stood. Grabbed her clutch bag. 'If you'll excuse me, I need the restroom.'

Then she left the table as if the hounds of hell were chasing her. Gage watched her go, watched the brisk walk, the way her hips swayed, moulded by the soft blue fabric of her dress as she was pointed in the right direction by the helpful waiter.

'Perhaps that conversation was indelicate of me. Eve's a charming woman and it must be distressing.'

'She sometimes forgets how cruel people can be. She's a sensitive soul, my fiancée.' He hesitated for a moment. It was the truth. How could he have forgotten that? She'd always seen the best in things and people, even when life had thrown up the worst.

But she'd looked shocked, truly shocked by the revelation, and his brain wouldn't let him process it. His life had been lived under the assumption she'd been complicit in all the attempts to ruin his reputation. He didn't know how to think any other way. It was his frame of reference for all his thoughts and beliefs about their relationship.

'I hope I haven't upset her.'

Eve's horrified tone, the blood draining from her face, all the colour gone. He couldn't stop thinking that this had been a complete surprise to her. What if it was? What if she'd had no idea at all, exiled as she'd been over here in France? He couldn't process any of it, it was as though his whole life had been upended. 'Perhaps I'll go and check…'

'You should. I'll sit here and continue to sample this delightful wine. We have much to discuss over the coming months, Gage,' Greta said enigmatically.

But somehow he couldn't see it as a triumph as he stood and left the table.

All he could think of was Eve, and how shattered she'd appeared.

CHAPTER SEVEN

EVE STOOD AT the basin, staring into the mirror. She took a deep breath, trying to calm her pounding heart, to ease the twist of pain. She'd never heard the rumours. How could anyone claim such an awful thing, that she hadn't gone willingly with Gage? She'd so badly wanted to be Gage's wife that nothing else had mattered, not even her family. She'd have travelled to the ends of the earth for him. And people were saying that he'd effectively kidnapped her?

But that wasn't the worst of it. It had been the look on his face as they'd been discussing it. Anger and certainty, as if he was convinced she *had* known. She lifted a trembling hand and brushed at the smudges under her eyes that no amount of concealer could hide. It had been impossible to sleep over the past few months with worry about the business, her family and then being around Gage. Some days she barely functioned, and yet she needed to go back out there.

Perform. Play a part when all she wanted to do was curl up into a tiny ball and weep.

She turned on the cold tap and ran her wrists under the bracing water. Closed her eyes and tried to steady her throbbing heart. Stop the tears falling. She'd done it once. Survived the worst. All alone, thousands of miles from home, in a small church with a tiny white coffin and only a priest to see her tears. She'd woven that pain into the tapestry of her life and moved forward. What was one more time?

'Let's do this,' she said to her reflection, gritting her teeth and straightening her spine. She wrenched open the bathroom door, head down, and smacked straight into a wall of hard muscle and chest. Hands clasped her arms to steady her. She didn't need to be afraid of who it was. She knew. That heat, the smell of the man that made her crave to nestle her head against all that strength and soak it into herself for a while.

Gage.

But if she did, she might never let him go and she would always have to leave. Still, she couldn't muster the will to fight him. Not right now. She leaned back and met his gaze. A slight crease in his forehead was the only sign of all the questions she could never answer written there. Something soft and unreadable in his eyes. It undid her. As if looking back at her was the twenty-three-year-old young man she'd loved and left. The billionaire businessman was gone.

'Are you okay?'

No one had ever asked that in all these years. The doctors had talked about scientific probabilities. Nurses had patted her arm and said she was young; she'd have another baby. The priest had talked about God's will. No one had asked about *her*. Of course she'd hidden it from her family, not wanting her father to rage at the knowledge that a Caron had touched his daughter. Not wanting any of them to express relief that her baby had been lost, because that would have broken her completely.

Not even her mom or sister had asked how she was coping with losing Gage. It was as if, for them, that part of her life had ceased to exist. When for her there had been no relief, only bottomless grief.

She had run a business and people had assumed she was okay. Her family had relied on her. No one had ever thought about what *she* wanted, *ever*. Except for Gage. Now he cupped her cheek because he could always see through her. Saw what others might miss. Part of her wished she could tell him what had happened, to share the pain, but what good would it do? It was better that he remain blissfully unaware. The burden was hers to carry. No one else's. And at that moment she let go. If he hadn't been steadying her, she would have fallen apart completely.

'The rumours. What were they exactly?'

His gaze hardened. 'You know.'

She shook her head almost hard enough to give herself vertigo. Tears pricked at her eyes. 'You have to believe me. I don't.'

'Wasn't what you heard enough? You didn't want to come with me. I forced you to. You were scared of me and had a lucky escape.'

She gripped at the fabric of his shirt, crushing it in her fingers. 'Who said those things?'

'I thought it was you.'

'Never!'

'Okay. Let's assume it wasn't you.' He didn't sound convinced and his frown remained. 'I can't believe you'd be so naïve as to not guess who else might have had a reason. There's only one possibility.'

No. Her father had promised Gage would be left alone. That had been their deal. He'd be left to live his life…and she'd try to pick up the pieces of hers. 'People make up stories all the time.'

'And still you defend him. Sure, people make up stories. But every time something great was happening with Caron, a quiet word and investors melted away. I had to fight harder than anyone to keep things going. These anonymous whispers only came out when it would do most damage. And who would want to hurt me if not you? Your father.'

She released the crushed cotton of Gage's shirt and buried her head in her hands. How could anyone sully the memory of that time? It had been terrifying, exciting, full of promise and hope for the future. That's what she remembered. And the sense of desperation that they had been each other's one and only, and no one could tear them apart. Once it had ended, clinging to the hope that what they'd both have left were beautiful memories, and for her that would be enough to survive on.

But to dirty their past this way was unforgivable, hitting deep at the heart of their young love. She'd always believed the deal she'd struck with her father. That she'd leave Gage, and nothing would be said about his family or what had happened. He'd *promised*.

'Who promised?'

She'd said that aloud? Part of her wanted to tell Gage, to shout that she'd never stopped loving him and had made a devil's bargain to protect him.

No wonder Gage hated her, wanted revenge, this charade of a relationship. Because someone had been dripping poison into people's ears about him for years, poisoning him in the process. Yet another thing she'd have to atone for and fix. Because she *would* fix this. She'd work day and night to repair the damage her father had done, even if it meant once again sacrificing herself.

'We should get back to Greta. She'll be wondering where we are.'

Gage cupped her cheeks and stared down at her in this dim corridor, trying to delve into her soul.

'You carry a world of pain in your eyes. I want to know why. What's hurting you?'

How could she answer?

Your dad's not really your father. You're someone else's son. I lost our baby.

She could say all those things. The secrets she'd held onto for years. But what good would it do to unburden them all now?

'Nothing, other than revisiting our past. I'm all for moving forward.'

He scanned her face, one corner of his mouth quirking up in a tiny smile.

'Why did I ever believe you were a good liar?' he murmured.

Because it was easy to lie when she wasn't standing in front of him. But this had been the flaw in agreeing to the deal to save Knight. Because the man in the flesh was her Kryptonite. She'd been a fool to think that she could carry through with this game. She always held the losing hand, craving his warmth and strength. Especially now. And maybe that was exactly something she could take, something to distract them both from the truths she could never tell. So she grabbed the lapels of his jacket as his eyes darkened. Went up further on her toes and pulled his head down to her lips.

Her kiss demanded hard and passionate, but their lips touched and all Gage gave was gentle. Arms sliding round her back, holding her with a kind of reverence she didn't deserve. His lips moved over hers, coaxing her to give more than she wanted to. And, still, she couldn't help falling into it. This kiss that whispered it was more about love than desire. Timeless and endless. Not like the stolen kisses of their youth but something older, wiser and infinitely more dangerous because it carried all the hurts of the past mingled with what felt a lot like forgiveness.

She was held safe, ensnared by all the slick and hypnotising rhythm of it. Never wanting the moment to end. And maybe even if she couldn't tell him how she felt, she was showing it here. But she was terrified that he was showing her something too. Gage's hand delved into her hair, holding her tight, giving and taking. His body was hot and hard against hers, his arousal obvious, making her want. The core of her ached, needing him to fill her. Then he slowed, pulled away, his breathing heavy.

'We need to go,' she said. She didn't look at him, because if she did it would likely end her.

'We're not done, Eve. This conversation isn't over.'

That didn't matter to her so long as it was over for now. Then she could pull herself together before she completely fell apart, because she held secrets Gage was never going to find out.

Eve and he had walked back to the table hand in hand. They'd finished up with Greta, and she'd promised to call Eve about the vineyard. It was everything he could have dreamed of, the deal not yet sealed but he was sure it would be. The whole thing had been so laughably easy it was almost an anti-climax to all that had gone before.

And yet the night felt as if something had irrevocably changed. All those years he'd believed that Eve had been a party to the insidious rumours about him and she was adamant she'd had no idea. Once he might not have believed her denials, had he not witnessed her reaction tonight. The shock, the horror was so genuine he doubted even the best actress could have played the part so well. It convinced him she'd had no idea at all.

If he'd been wrong about that, what else had he been wrong about? Gage couldn't fathom the possibilities. He'd suffered through that excruciating phone call when he'd promised to take Eve away from her family, when she'd viciously rejected his love, treating him like a foolish boy. The scorn in her voice. That had all been painfully real. The question now, all these years on, was why had she done it?

For seven years he'd been certain of where he stood in the world. Now he wasn't sure of anything. In the back of the car, on the way home to Grasse, Eve had pressed herself so far against the door on the other side of the car it had been as though she was in another country. Why had she been so far away? That kiss she'd given him had rocked his foundations. Something he wanted to explore because he was sure she'd used it to distract him from getting to the truth. As if it would have all spilled out if she'd allowed herself to get close.

The car travelled up the long farmhouse drive and halted at the front doors. As Gage thanked the driver Eve jumped out of the car, almost fleeing to the door, except tonight she didn't have the key. He strolled towards her, formulating his plan because this night wasn't ending here. Eve was still like a drug flowing through his veins and he craved more of her.

'Have a drink with me,' he said.

'I think I've had more than enough tonight.' Her voice was soft, a little breathy. He knew that tone, the one that told him how much she desired him. In all this time he hadn't forgotten the things that made her tick.

'I'd like to discuss the dinner, see if there's anything I've missed.'

Business. He gave her that to hide behind. She sighed, and the sound of it caressed him like a feather down his spine.

'Now?'

'While it's fresh.' Gage pushed the door open. 'Come into the kitchen.' She'd think that was neutral space, whereas he saw no part of this place as neutral. It was all a war zone, one way or another, and he'd never been known to lose a battle.

He followed Eve through the house, the scent of her trailing behind like that of the fields of flowers surrounding this place. As they entered the kitchen, with its stone walls and exposed wooden beams, he could see how this home suited the very core of her. Except right now she didn't seem comfortable here, edging around the counter area and away from him. She dragged out a barstool and sat, slipping off her stilettos.

Pink. Her toenails were a pretty pink.

'Would you like warm milk, bourbon and honey to help you sleep?' He went to the refrigerator.

'Sure, why not?'

She sounded like he'd just asked her to chew glass.

'I'd appreciate your opinion on how tonight went.'

He didn't give a damn about the drink or the dinner. Greta was on board. They'd have to play a few more rounds of getting to know each other but Greta had liked what she'd seen. All that he cared about now was the woman sitting in front of him. Because after what he'd learned tonight, everything was *not* as it seemed.

As he mechanically grabbed what he needed and began preparing the nightcap, Eve sat there, working through her observations. They were insightful and damned clever. Proving herself to be the businesswoman she'd claimed to have become. No longer a precious society princess or trust-fund child.

Once he'd believed she'd been given the job in France out of nepotism. He'd bet now that she'd been sent here to keep her away from him. Gage finished making the sweet, milky concoction with a solid slug of spirits and poured cups for them both. Eve took a generous sip and didn't even blink at the amount of bourbon in the cup. He wondered whether she often had trouble sleeping and how much she used this particular remedy.

'Of course, with Greta set to invest, you won't need me soon,' Eve said. That jolted him right back into what had been a one-sided conversation.

'She's invited us to her party in Munich in a few months. We're not done till that deal is signed.'

Eve fished her phone from her bag, flicked through a few screens. Hesitated.

'I see we've hit the press. What a sweet picture you've painted.' Her voice burned as caustic as lye. But he stopped listening to the words and went back to watching the woman. She wasn't looking at her phone anymore but at her engage-ment ring, which she twisted to catch the light. 'I assume you have a plan for when we end it. Something suitably nebulous, like work keep-ing us apart? A respectful uncoupling?'

No. He'd planned on dialling things up to ther-monuclear. A story that told the world exactly what sort of woman she was. A liar. But that didn't suit him now because he wasn't sure what she was. Still, he smiled, humoured her.

'Something like that.'

She looked at him with her china-blue eyes soft and with a wash of something else that, if he had to guess, looked like regret. He didn't want to talk about endings at all. He wanted to talk about beginnings. Reconnections. The things that lit a fire inside her because he loved her glow. He looked around the rustic farm-house kitchen, with Eve at its heart. Her corn-silk curls gleamed like an ethereal halo under the soft lights. She looked right, here in this place. Like she should be nowhere else.

'You must find the farm hard to leave.'

Eve raised her eyebrows and took another sip of her drink. He might have taken some of his too but he didn't want to go to sleep and he didn't need to be intoxicated. He was man enough to admit she did that to him already. She smiled, something soft and mysterious that lit her up from inside.

'It is. I try to stay here whenever it's not rented out, which isn't often enough.'

'Why rent it out at all?'

She shrugged. 'I have a loan I want to pay off faster and tourists are happy to pay a premium to stay here. I do what I have to do.'

'And when you don't need to anymore?'

'I'll come here and stand on the back terrace, overlooking *my* fields, smelling the roses and lavender on the breeze. And I'll never leave.' A blush rose on her face, as beautiful as the sun breaking over the horizon at dawn. 'It's silly, really. Following the seasons. Sitting back and watching things grow.'

He drank some of the bourbon mixture, grimaced. Turned out this was *not* one of the things he enjoyed.

'There's nothing silly about it. It's always been your dream.' Gage noticed there was no talk of relationships or family. He didn't know why that left him with a pang of something like sadness.

The simple things he'd once loved were all

tied up with memories of Eve. Sneaking off and meeting through that hole in the wall. Threading flowers into her hair so she looked like some ethereal fairy princess, all golden and beautiful. When she'd rejected him, he'd stopped dreaming of simple, even frivolous things and had driven himself in a never-ending quest to redeem his name. It had been exhausting. What a pleasure it would have been to merely sit somewhere and look at a landscape. To…stop.

'It wasn't my only dream once,' Eve said. Her gaze met his. There was so much unsaid, and he couldn't seem to find the words to pick a way through the maze of the past that stood between them. 'What's yours?'

He should have said the deal with Greta Bonitz. That's what he'd wanted more than anything only weeks before, but he couldn't say that because it would be a lie now. His dreams were shifting things, dredging up fantasies held so long ago they'd been forgotten. Of marriage, children. Old desires he'd tried to cast aside, along with the painful memories.

The sad truth was his dreams were still tied up in her.

'You,' he said with no plan or forethought,

leaving himself open to attack. He didn't care if what came next left his blood on the floor. He needed to get to the bottom of what was going on here.

Eve grabbed her cup and clutched it on her lap in both hands. Not looking at him now but into her drink. Her lower lip trembled till she sank her teeth into it. For a few moments he worried she might draw blood.

'No. I can't be your dream. I'm your nightmare.'

'My dreams are my own. Sure, they've become nightmares because I shouldn't touch you. But in my fantasies... I can do anything.' He moved around the counter to where she sat, still resolutely avoiding his gaze. 'Do you fantasise too? Maybe about me untying that distracting bow at your hip? Teasing those tight nipples I can see right now through your dress. Undoing you. Is that what you're fantasising about?'

He ached for her, but this was a long game he played now. Gage reached out and brushed the tangle of her golden locks over Eve's shoulder. The drink in her cup quivered. She gave an imperceptible shake of her head. 'I'm tired.'

If he had his way, there'd be no sleep in this

house tonight. A heavy pulse beat low and insistently in him. 'I can think of better ways of getting to sleep than milk and bourbon. Let me show you.'

Her lips parted, the death-like grip on her cup loosening a fraction. He grabbed the rim and eased it out of her hands.

'What are you doing?'

Her voice was low and husky. A flush ran up her throat. She knew exactly what he was doing. He cupped her cheek, stroked his thumb against her smooth, soft skin. Eve finally looked at him, her eyes bottomless pools, almost all pupil surrounded by a sliver of pale blue.

'I'm going to kiss you,' he said, the anticipatory pleasure surging through him making him hard, desperate, when he needed infinite patience tonight. He leaned down to whisper in her ear, 'Then I'm going to carry you to my room. Peel that tempting dress from your glorious body.' The panting of her breath teased at his neck. 'I'm going to caress, kiss, explore every part of you.' He skimmed his lips feather-light along her throat. 'And only when you're trembling, wet and mad with desire will I make love to you. For hours. I want to hear you scream my name. Over and over.'

He skimmed his lips over the side of her neck, past the base of her ear. His eyes drifted shut as his nose brushed her cheek. 'Say yes, *cher*, and I'm yours for tonight.'

He wanted more than a night, but Eve was afraid of something and if she thought their time was limited she might just let go of that tight control...enough. She twined her arm around his neck and pressed her lips to his. Her lips parting. Their tongues touching.

There was nothing bold about her, just uncertainty. Something about that, how tentative they were at this moment, made him feel young again. Like the world had possibility rather than being full of disappointment. He wanted her here. Now. On this cold marble counter. The drive to tear off the dress and lay her out rode him hard. But he'd told her his plans and wouldn't deviate from the promises he'd made her. He kissed her back, relishing in the softness of her mouth, the hesitant stroke of her tongue. Let himself believe they were back...before. Before any of the pain and hurt. He pulled away from her and looked down, her lips dark pink and moist, her breaths heavy, matching his.

'Bed.'

'Yes.'

He swung her into his arms, where she clung on, so light and breakable. Something precious to be cosseted and adored. She nuzzled into his neck as he carried her to his room, striding with purpose, in a hurry to get there because the night ahead loomed large and pleasure-filled. He'd have her again, and again and again. Hell, he needed to take a few breaths to make sure he'd last. Even the thought of being inside her once more unravelled him. He walked through the door of his room into darkness. Found the bed and gently laid her on the covers then moved away.

'Where are you going?' Eve asked, voice low as if whispering some naughty secrets.

'A light. I want to see you.'

'No!' Her voice was strident, a strange discord in the evening. 'I... I want you now. Like this. Don't leave me.'

The blood surged through him again. That wasn't something he could ignore and now his eyes had adjusted to the lower light he glimpsed the way the moon glowing through the expansive French doors cast her in its silver light.

'Whatever the lady desires, she shall have.' He moved to her dress. That bow at her side, which had been plaguing him all night. He plucked at the end of the tie, ever so slowly, pulling as the loop of the bow slipped through. He eased apart the remains of the knot and peeled the dress open. She lay splayed on the fabric, her body pale, her bra and panties a dark trace of lace on her moonlit body.

He craved to see those breasts again without a bra. To taste them, toy with her nipples till she writhed in ecstasy. Something wild and possessive grabbed him, wanting her to beg him to satisfy her. To prove she should never have left him. To prove that no one else could ever give her what he had.

As much as desire drove him to tear off her clothes and pound into her like a crazed man, he wouldn't. Her rapid breaths were like music in the air. He eased her panties down her legs and tossed the flimsy lace to the floor. Leaned over her, stroked his fingers whisper-light up her leg till she shivered and moaned, then dropped his head and kissed the soft, pale skin of her stomach, lower and lower. Breathing in the scent of her sweet arousal. He hovered for a moment, one hand stroking, his breath on the juncture of her thighs because he wasn't ashamed to admit he wanted her too. He was aching and hard, his clothes gripping him too tight.

Eve squirmed underneath him. 'Please.'

He smiled. Kissed his way up her body. Settled his lips over her left nipple, already a hard peak, and sucked it through the lace of her bra. Her groan was deep and carnal and sliced through him with shards of anticipatory pleasure.

Gage pulled down the other cup of her bra, twirled her free nipple between his fingers as Eve reached her hands and grappled with the buttons on his shirt. He loved her desperate, staccato movements, her frantic tugs at the fabric, pulling it from his trousers.

'Too many clothes,' she groaned. He shrugged the shirt from his body and threw it to the side. Undid his belt and whipped it from his trousers.

'Get rid of this damned bra.' He kissed the side of her neck as she rolled to one side and he undid the clasp at the back, freeing her. He sat back on his haunches, looking down at her body in the cool light. Sprawled out on the bed with her hair feathered on the pillow. Her features were smudged and blurred like a charcoal portrait in the soft light. Gage dropped his head again, kissing her perfect breasts. Laying his body over Eve and relishing in the contrast of her softness to his hardness, her edges and angles underneath him.

He didn't care that he still had his trousers on. If he took them off, this would be over too soon. Eve wrapped her legs around him, ground her body against his hardness as he captured her lips in his own, their kisses wet and frantic with nipping teeth. He wanted to see that, see her lips, swollen and well kissed, and know that he had done that. Wrecked her, like she was wrecking him. Her legs gripped tighter as he lost himself in the grind of their bodies, plucking at her nipples with his fingers, tongues exploring, their movements in such synchronicity it was like they'd never been apart.

She pulled her mouth away. 'I need you.'

The bright burst of arousal tore through him, his body heavy with it. Aching. 'I know,' he murmured against her lips. He rolled to the side, his trousers now an impediment. He reached for the zip.

Eve rolled to the side too. 'Let me.' She slid the zipper down all too slowly, reached her hand into his trousers and gripped his length through his underwear. He dropped his head back. Relished her touch. She slipped below the waistband of his briefs. Stroked him with her cool, firm touch and he almost shot off the bed at the shock. It was his turn to groan, throw back his head. Take. Savour.

Her firm fingers rubbed over the tip, working him like he'd shown her he enjoyed so many years ago. But this wasn't about him as the prickle at the base of his spine sounded a warning, the heaviness that told him he'd lose control soon. It was about her, breaking her apart.

He moved off the bed and looked down at her, unable to judge her expression in the darkness. He stripped himself of his trousers, underwear and knelt on the bed, dropping his head to the juncture of her thighs. Breathed in her sweet musky scent.

She spread her legs wider, fell open for him as he traced her with his tongue, relishing the salty sweet taste unique to her. He delved between her legs. Concentrated on the tight little bud and made her squirm and moan, lavishing her with attention. He slipped his hand between her thighs, probing her wet depths as he slid one finger inside then another and curled them to hit the spot he knew drove her wild.

Her back arched. She gripped the sheets, her thighs trembling as he lapped at her body, taking her higher and higher, but he wouldn't let her fall yet. He eased off a touch, bringing her back down. He could make this pleasure last for hours if he wanted to. He knew all about delayed gratification and patience. He had warned her after all.

Her hands released the sheets and one thrust into his hair, gripping tight. He relished the bite of pain, the desperation it showed.

'All of you.' Her voice was like the slip of lace over beautiful curves. As soft as the moonlight caressing her body. 'Inside me. *Please.*'

He'd wanted to hear her beg but it didn't hold the pleasure he'd thought it would. He needed to be inside her, to slide into her hot, wet depths and lose himself right along with her.

'Yes.' He rolled over and opened the bedside drawer.

'*No,*' Eve said, and he halted immediately, a sinking feeling hitting his stomach. She'd changed her mind? She reached out her arms and tried to pull him back to her. 'Only you. Nothing between us. Just you inside me.'

The rush was like a drug. Like being hit, hard. In all the time since Eve he'd never had sex without a condom. The only time he ever had was with her that long-ago morning.

'I trust you. I need you.'

And that's all it took, the expression of trust so heady he almost came then and there without her hands even on his body. He didn't care anymore. He rolled over onto her, settled between her glorious thighs. Positioned himself and hesitated for a second before slowly pushing home. His mind blanked. The white-hot spike of pleasure almost undid him. Eve gripped his body hard. He hesitated for a moment.

'Good?' He ground out the word through gritted teeth because this was better than good. Just having her underneath him, being inside her, felt life-altering.

'Yes.' Her voice was barely a whisper and then he began to thrust, long and slow, a hypnotic rhythm of push and pull. Her lips on his, tongue exploring his mouth. All slick and wet and barely controlled. She moved with him; her legs wrapped around his. Meeting him with every thrust. Moments of exquisite sensation that had him thanking the heavens she'd allowed him back into her body again. He didn't care right now what had come before, only this moment, pure and perfect.

The grind of her against him, the movements not so controlled now, told him she was close. She chased her pleasure and he was happy to give it to her. He dropped his head and sucked on her nipple as she tensed then splintered around him. Crying out his name. He buried his head into the side of her throat, breathing in the sweet scent of her hair as she brought herself up to meet him and gripped hard. He knew she was going to come again and held out for as long as he could till she grabbed his backside hard and dug her nails in deep. She could draw blood and he didn't care. A bright burst of light exploded in his head as he tumbled over the edge. Her sobbing cries announced she'd gone over with him, again. And as the world righted itself, he heard the whisper he was sure she'd never meant him to hear. Three words that changed everything.

'Only ever you.'

CHAPTER EIGHT

MORNINGS WERE FOR reckoning, and Eve wondered how swift that reckoning would be today. She'd woken to a body aching, sated and boneless. But her heart and soul weren't sated. They'd never get enough of this. The touches in the darkness, the furtive kisses. The screaming want that would never go away.

And this morning the fantasies in the darkness collided with the brutal reality of the daytime. What had she said last night? Hidden by the moonlight, it seemed as if any of her most furtive imaginings could be real. That time could be turned back, and she and Gage could pretend they were in their early twenties again, when anything had seemed possible.

So little was possible now, all their history wound up with secrets. She should get up, move. Leave this bed and this room and flee, and to hell with everything. Her family, the company. This, here, was risking her soul and she didn't think she had enough strength to keep the charade going any longer.

'Morning.' Gage's midnight voice didn't suit the sunshine filtering into the room through gauzy curtains. It spoke of the night, of twisted sheets and whispered caresses that could be hidden. In the daylight there was nowhere to hide.

'Morning back at you.'

In moments her world flipped, and she found herself rolled over and underneath a hot, hard body. Any thoughts of getting up and running away evaporated in a welling of need. She shifted under him and winced. It had been a long, passionate night with little sleep, but her aches eased, to be replaced by another—the hot slide of desire working low down. There was no ending to how much she craved this man.

'Are you hurting?' His voice sounded so gentle. The look on his face concerned. It was worrying, this time spent with him. He was less the hard businessman, more the generous lover. Someone dangerous in every sense to her health and happiness. He pushed himself further up on his elbows and looked down at her, as if checking.

'A few aches and pains.' She shrugged, trying for a nonchalance she didn't feel. 'As I said, it's been a while.'

His eyes darkened to the blue of a stormy sea. His pupils almost swallowed any colour.

'How long?'

Gage's voice was soft, the question sounding innocent enough, and yet a thread ran through it, something dark and dangerous. It felt important and screamed a kind of warning. She'd broken open, leaving herself vulnerable in a way she hadn't allowed for years. Words had spilled out of her like she'd been given a truth serum, and while most of them could have been excused as being whispered in the throes of passion, the heat of the moment, some couldn't. She'd hoped he hadn't noticed, but with Gage she'd never really had room to hide. This soft and caring man unravelled her every time. She looked away.

'Long enough.'

Why couldn't she say something sophisticated, urbane? Something a woman experienced in having great sex would say. Something to shut him down rather than crack the door open even wider.

'Last night you said—'

'Sugar, I say a lot of things when I'm chasing an orgasm.' She would not let him use her words against her. Not words spoken in the heat of the moment. 'Don't believe everything you hear.'

She covered the lie well enough and what she'd said was designed to be brutal. She could deal with him angry. It's what she wanted. Safer that way for her and for him. But the words left a sour taste in her mouth, felt tainted, because last night had been something special and beautiful.

She expected him to pull away in disgust, to leave the bed. Instead he settled down, over her. His gaze might have changed fleetingly, a tightness that she couldn't read, but he didn't shift. His forearms remained either side of her head, his thumbs stroking at her hairline. She wanted to close her eyes, to soak in the gentleness and the caring, but that would leave her exposed again.

'I'm coming to realise what I should believe and what I shouldn't,' he said, skimming his lips over her mouth. The whole of her flooded with a slick heat. She didn't care that she ached, she revelled in his hard body against hers. If they made love again, he'd forget this, they could lose themselves in pleasure and he wouldn't ask the hard questions anymore.

When Gage's lips descended on hers, she captured them, the kiss soft and coaxing. He groaned and the sound punched right through her. He was hard against her, aroused again with that one kiss and the tangle of their tongues, and she threaded her hands through his hair, widening her legs and rolling her hips against him. He was in the perfect position to slide easily inside her and carry them away to bliss again, but he didn't, just let her grind against him till they were both panting and desperate. Then he adjusted his position and she sighed at the feel of him easing inside her. He whispered words in her ear that had her melting. *'The feel of you against me. So perfect. Never wanted this so much.'*

And she wanted it too. She wanted it all.

The impossible. *Everything.*

Tears pricked her eyes. Maybe she could lie about why she'd ended what they'd had, but then this would be like a house of cards, bound to blow over in a rough breeze. With their families loathing each other, there would be plenty of those. Better they remain here in a physical relationship and that was all. The sensation built inside her, that glorious burn, a wave of pleasure that she'd soon ride to oblivion so she could forget everything but his touch.

Except Gage pulled back, threaded his fingers in hers and raised her hands above her head, trapped her. His thrusts were gentle and shallow and avoided the contact she craved. His eyes were intent on her, so blue it hurt to look at them.

'Look at you. So beautiful underneath me.'

She arched her back but he wouldn't let her finish, watching her writhe against him. 'Gage. Please.'

'I love seeing you want me so badly.'

A sheen of sweat misted his skin. The room was warm from the morning sunshine hitting the glass as he kept up the slow, relentless rhythm that wouldn't let her finish.

'Memories taunted me for years and now I have you.'

She arched back, groaned. 'I need.'

'I know.' And yet he didn't relieve the ache, it only intensified. She chased the pressure, him grinding against her. His hand. Anything other than this torture. But he didn't relent. 'I'll make you scream if you answer.'

Her body was wound so tight she thought she would tear apart. She trembled underneath him. 'Anything,' she panted. Closed her eyes because if she concentrated hard enough she might get there, with or without him. But he eased off even more and that delicious fall over the edge remained just out of reach.

'How long?' he murmured. She tried to ignore the question but she couldn't as the sharp bite of pleasure went on and on. Gage leaned down and grazed his teeth on the shell of her ear. 'How long has it been since someone's touched you like this?'

Only him.

She shook now. Their bodies coming together but never enough for her. He knew what it took to get her over the edge, that hadn't changed. Her body hadn't learned anything different because he'd been her only lover. In her own guilty explorations after they'd parted, all she'd been able to think of had been him. She'd tried to imagine sex with anyone else, but no one other than Gage entered her fantasies. Now he was denying her and she didn't care about secrets. All she wanted was him.

'Don't be afraid, *cher.*'

Tears burned her eyes and ran down her cheeks. Tears of frustration and need, sure, but more at the loss of this. All the years they'd missed.

She opened her eyes and he looked down at her, his gaze searching her face. His golden hair had fallen over his forehead and his eyes were intent, as if he could see everything like he'd used to—her hopes, dreams, fears. So many fears. And for a few moments she wanted to give him a truth so it could set her free. She'd stitch herself up with lies later.

'Seven years.'

Seven long, lonely, devastating years. A look scudded across his face, a thousand thoughts hidden there, all of which were unreadable. Then he pulled away. She was left empty and aching.

'*No*. That's not—'

'You promised,' she sobbed.

He hesitated then kissed the middle of her chest, lingering over where her heart pounded. 'And I keep my promises.' He kissed her navel, trailed his tongue down lower, and lower. 'I'll look after you.' His breath was a warm caress between her legs. He lingered for a few moments then dropped his head. 'I always will.'

Gage stroked his tongue over the centre of her. That's all it took to make her scream and lose herself in the promise she could never allow him to keep.

CHAPTER NINE

THE MORE THINGS appeared to have changed, the more Gage realised they'd stayed the same. Except life wasn't imbued with the innocence of seven years ago. It had been tainted by something unknown, lurking in the shadows. A brooding monster he'd try to get to the bottom of, if Eve would let him.

She lay sleeping in his arms, where she'd been for a few hours now after turning his world on its head with one truth. Now he was frozen at the information she'd disclosed. Like a sliver of glass in the sole of his foot, the thought stabbed at him. Seven years. As if time hadn't moved on for her at all. He'd thought she didn't want him, that her trust fund or marriage to a society prince was all she'd sought, with him a toy along the way to play with. He'd been convinced that he wasn't good enough, and yet in all that time there'd been no one else for her.

She could be lying, but he knew deep down

that she wasn't. The question was, why? He would get to the bottom of it, but telling him seemed to cost her a great deal so he allowed her a break, letting her sleep while his thoughts whirred. He couldn't escape the realisation that the choice to reject him might not have been hers. What threats had been made against her? What had been done to turn their love into this twisted charade?

The burning heat of rage threatened to ignite in his gut. All this time. The wasted years. For what? And whoever was responsible, they'd pay. He'd get to the bottom of what happened, and then burn it all down.

Eve stirred. An elegant stretch of her body as she gently woke in his arms. Parts of him stirred with her. He could tell the moment she realised where she was. Her body, previously languid and soft, now stiffened and moved away from him. She looked at him, the barest of creases between her brows, her eyes watchful. He hated that, the uncertainty in them.

Once they'd been certain of each other. He craved that certainty again. He brushed a soft kiss over her lips and gloried in the pink flush that bloomed over her skin. He didn't want to break the moment, but he needed answers. And he needed to ask the questions carefully. But Eve continued to distance herself from him.

'When are we leaving for the US?' she asked, her voice husky from sleep.

'Keen to get home?' *Home.* That word held a tantalising hint of what might have been between them. Building a haven against the world. What still could be, if he allowed himself to be honest...

'America hasn't been home for a long time.' Eve's fingers tortured the sheets. 'No. I can't get any information about my father. Mom and Veronique aren't making any sense about what's going on.'

It was as if someone had thrown a bucket of iced water over him. Gage resented mention of Hugo Chevalier entering the hallowed space of this shared bed. He breathed through the ever-present burn of anger that the man still had some malevolent power over Eve.

'I'll check flight arrangements. I've got some things to tie up in Mississippi first, before we head back to Seattle.' Except every part of him railed against leaving here, a sickening knot in his gut only getting tighter. As if reality would intrude and nothing would be the same again.

She nodded, looking far away. 'I should get up and—'

'There's no hurry.' He didn't want her getting out of the bed and leaving, not yet, when so many questions needed answering. 'Why, Eve?'

Her mouth firmed to a tight line. 'I don't know what—'

'Yes, you do. Why has there been no one else? Seven years is a long time.'

Her closing down to him began right then, the shuttering behind her eyes clear, like she'd pulled down a blind and excluded him from the room.

'I was studying and then thrown into managing the business here.'

The lie was written all over her face. The way her eyes avoided his. The way her throat convulsed as she swallowed. Her words sounded genuine but the look of her screamed volumes. If he'd been able to see her face to face in their final conversation, would he have seen the truth? Because all he'd heard had been the words, and he suspected now that those words had been blatant lies too.

'You're a beautiful, passionate woman. Men would have flocked to you.' They would have wanted her. He'd taunted himself for enough years with thoughts of her and any man other than him, till he'd hardened his heart to granite. Nothing and no one had been let in since.

She shrugged. Wriggled away. She still wouldn't look at him and all he saw was embarrassment and a spark of something else, hot and angry, in the flare of her pale blue eyes.

'Men did, but I had *focus*. Something to achieve. I'd been given a job to do here, and I excelled at it. I didn't need the attentions of a random man to make me feel good about myself.'

She rolled over and almost threw herself from the bed in her haste to escape. Glorious. Naked. He wanted to drag her back like some caveman, spend hours buried in her till they had to leave for their flight. Although it was tempting to skip it altogether and stay, continue the fantasy that they could remain cocooned from the outside world.

'Come back to bed. I won't ask any more questions. Let me make love to you instead.'

Her eyes softened for a moment. He drew

back the sheet and patted the mattress beside him. There'd be no mistaking how badly he wanted her, and if Eve didn't want questions asked for now, he could do that.

Eve's gaze raked his body like her nails had scored his skin. Flares of heat ignited where it lingered. His face, chest, lower and then her pupils flared wide and dark. He smiled because he had her, and she knew it. They could resist many things, but not each other. He held out his hand to her. 'C'mon. You're not scared, are you?'

'Nothing scares me anymore,' she said in a husky whisper.

He reached out and she placed her hand in his. He tugged and she tumbled onto the bed and into his arms. Their truth screamed loudly in every touch and caress when they were in bed, tangled together. Here there were no lies between them, only raw honesty. If this was all Eve had to give for now, that would be enough.

Eve slept through most of the flight. The long, passionate night when they'd made love over and over, taking its delectable toll. It was as though they were trying to exorcise the demons of the past, as though when buried in each other they could regain something they'd lost.

She allowed it, the fantasy that this could last, because she'd come to the blinding realisation that she'd never stopped loving Gage. She now knew it was why she rarely returned to the US, to the place where they'd begun. She'd stayed in France and video-called the family. Had attended obligatory holidays when her presence had been unavoidable—Christmas, Thanksgiving—and only when internet alerts had told her that Gage was somewhere else so there'd been no chance of ever bumping into one another.

Now, in a car on the soil of the place she'd once believed was home, her anxiety ratcheted higher. Eve took some slow, steady breaths. Checked her phone. Still no real word about her father, just some bland-sounding messages from her mom and sister about him improving and coming out of ICU.

'I thought you'd have an apartment here,' she said as they pulled up outside an anonymous boutique hotel where a doorman waited for them.

Gage shook his head, gazing out the window,

his mouth narrowed to a tight, hard line. 'I'm not here often enough for somewhere permanent. On the rare occasions I stay, it's at the guesthouse at Mom and Dad's. I didn't think you'd want to go there.'

He was right, but for reasons Gage would never know. That place carried too many memories of the night they'd been foolish and had lacked caution just before they'd run. The night she'd fallen pregnant.

She shoved that thought down into the recesses of her memory where it silently taunted her, and exited into the cool, rarefied air. She held her breath as their bags were taken from the car. Even though the bellhop was careful with their luggage, her small, battered yellow suitcase wasn't treated with as much reverence as it deserved.

Usually she didn't allow anyone else to touch it. It didn't feel right. That one small case held all the wounds of her past. She flexed her fingers. Itched to go retrieve it. Ignored the sensation. Gage had looked at her oddly when she'd demanded she carry it onto the plane herself. There had been too many questions on his face. She didn't want them asked of her.

In the lift to their room Gage grabbed her. Pressed her up against the cool, mirrored wall. Dropped his lips to hers hard, in a kiss that took and conquered. Desperate, as if being here would tear them apart again if they didn't reconnect immediately. She gave in to it, wiping away the memories of being back here. The place that had seen the beginning and the end of them.

They entered the suite, all warm neutrals that said nothing. Their bags would be up soon. She walked through, put down her tote on the plump couch and stared out the window at a city that now seemed foreign to her.

'I should see my family.' She hadn't wanted to mention it because she knew the hatred that ran deep, but she couldn't avoid the inevitable. Her father would know by now, if he was well enough, about Gage. About Knight. But if the man was conscious, she needed to see him, to reset the boundaries of their agreement. Ensure that the secrets he'd promised would be kept dead for ever.

'I know. Has there been any more news on your father?'

She turned away from the view she had no real interest in to look at Gage. His face gave away little. Not anger, or hatred. Nothing but acceptance.

'Not as much as I'd like...' She'd asked to speak to Hugo and the only message she'd received back had been from her mom: *'Reap what you sow...'* 'I suppose you'll want to see your mom and dad too?'

'They're away right now.' He hesitated for a moment, enough for her to notice. 'We can visit when they get back.'

A cold prickle of dread ran down her spine. It was as if everything was slowly escaping her control. Already Gage seemed to be incorporating her into his life. Even though this was fake, meeting his family as his fiancée *meant* something, she knew it. And how could she face them, knowing what she did? She thought about calling his parents. Demanding they speak with Gage, tell him the truth. But weren't some things their secrets to keep? Did Gus Caron even know himself? It was too much. What she needed wasn't a confrontation but time...

'I don't think that's a good idea.'

'Why?' That question. One word. So innocuous, when her answer could leave her exposed.

'I'm wondering how you're going to explain things when it all ends.'

'Thinking of me, *cher*?'

Always. 'I don't want to make things more difficult for you than they have to be.'

'I'm an adult, I can take responsibility for my own decisions.'

'What if I disappoint them?'

'You told me you weren't scared.'

'I'm not.'

Gage cocked his head as if he was about to say something but a knock at the door interrupted his response. He let the porter into the room with their bags. The man dealt with the larger cases and left the small ones for them. Gage thanked him. Gave him a generous tip. She moved to grab her yellow suitcase, to place it somewhere safe. Maybe the back of a wardrobe where it could be hidden from Gage's questioning gaze. Gage snagged it at the same time as she did. She jumped at the shock of his warm hand touching hers as they held the little case between them.

'I can take it,' he said.

She shook her head. He was so close to the truth about everything with his fingers on the handle. He let go as she pulled a little too hard and the latch gave. Her heart jolted to her throat as her life for the past seven years spilled onto the carpet in sheaves of paper and scrapbooks. She let go of the handle and the case tumbled with a thud to the floor.

'*No.*' She bent down, scrambling to snatch everything up, her frantic fingers ineffective at sweeping the scattered papers into a pile and away. Gage bent down to help and her mind blanked as he picked up a scrapbook that had fallen open. The articles she'd collected over the years. Most were on her computer but those she'd found in hard copy she'd carefully cut out and glued onto now yellowed pages. She'd followed Gage's every success and failure with an obsession, to make sure her sacrifice had been worth it. And it had, or so she'd thought.

He flicked through, hesitating on some pages. Picked up another. Seven years of news about him, all collected and curated. His gaze met hers. A frown on his face. His mouth opened, closed. Confusion. She snatched the book from his fingers.

'That's not yours to look at.'

'If not me, then who? Because it's all *about*

me. You collected…' His voice choked as he waved his hand over the remaining pages, lying about the carpeted floor like autumn leaves. She spied the corner of an official document, stowed in a plastic sleeve. One that had the power to tear the lies of the past seven years apart.

'So what if I did?'

'So *what*? You told me… You said… And yet you've been collecting articles about me. You didn't forget. You didn't put us behind you. Why?'

She gritted her teeth. Steeled herself for untruths to hide even greater secrets. This had to end now. 'We were too young. It would never have worked long term. Better the recriminations then than divorce lawyers now.'

'No.' He wouldn't stop looking at the papers on the floor, now running his hands through them, sorting, shifting. 'I do *not* believe you had so little faith in us.'

Eve didn't know what to do. She trembled, fighting back the tears threatening to fall.

'Stop.'

Gage didn't look up. He didn't acknowledge her at all and then there it was. Safely pressed into a journal. The midwife working at the hospital had done it for her. Tiny footprints and handprints in blue, from a soul who had come too early and left too soon. Gage held them for a few seconds before they slipped from his fingers, the precious papers falling back to the carpet to join the rest. He scrabbled through what remained until he came to the printed official French document.

Eve froze to the spot. She couldn't do anything but kneel there and watch the past years of their lives unravel like a skein of wool.

Because their son had breathed, he had a birth certificate. Louis Gage Chevalier. A name they'd always loved. Louis for a boy, Catherine for a girl. They'd dreamed every dream when they'd spun those fantasies with one another, when they'd been barely out of childhood themselves.

'A… a baby?' He scanned the page, looked at her, scanned it again. The paper shaking in his hands, '*Our* baby?'

'Yes.' Tears she'd promised she wouldn't cry anymore began sliding down her cheeks.

The heat of banked anger flared in Gage's eyes. 'How could you keep our son…*my* son…?'

She bit her lip hard to try and quell the pain

with something physical but the sharp bite did nothing to ease the hurt that had never quite healed, like a constant bruise. A lifetime was still too soon. But their child deserved to be finally known and acknowledged by someone other than her. And if Gage knew, maybe he'd stop asking questions that would lead to the most important secret of all she kept from him. A secret that was becoming harder to keep as time slid by.

'I didn't realise I was pregnant, not at first.' The stress, the heartbreak. Not eating, not sleeping. They'd all taken a toll and she hadn't put together what it meant when she'd missed her period. 'And when I did… You can't imagine.'

Being in France made it easier but she'd been terrified that someone would find out. Her father would have lost his mind if he'd known, and she'd already hurt Gage too much. In the beginning it had been what had driven her to succeed, to study and put everything behind her because she'd needed to keep secret the child she carried. At least for a while till she could plan, because after what she'd said to Gage it would have killed her if he'd questioned who the father was or, even worse, denied their baby.

'Where the hell *is* he?'

She couldn't say the words. Instead Eve gently sifted through the detritus of her life lying scattered on the floor. She found the document she was looking for and gave it to him. Whilst he might not be able to understand all that was written on the page, he'd recognize what it meant. Another official paper that had marked the end of all her dreams.

'I finally saw a doctor and it was going okay. Then at twenty-three weeks, it didn't.' She couldn't express the hope that had died then. It had felt like she had too, and a new Eve Chevalier had been carved from the winter of all that grief. Colder. Harder. The softness pared out of her. 'He was born so small. They tried to save him and he fought so hard, but...' She shook her head. In the days after that she'd become a zombie. The emotions too big to suffer alone and yet there was no alternative. Trying to hide what had happened because she'd been determined no one would ever find out.

'You should have said. I would have...' The look of anguish in his eyes as their worlds crumbled before them, all the things she'd hidden stitched tightly inside. Gage had that way of unpicking them one by one. 'Why didn't you tell me? Were you ever going to?'

'I was terrified.' At least that was a small part of why she'd done what she'd done. 'Scared of what my father would do.' If he'd known, he would have told Gage the truth about his parentage. She remembered that time of fear. Carrying Gage's child. Wanting to protect him, wanting to sort out the risks for them all in her heart before she announced to the world she was pregnant and the father was Gage.

'That man.' Gage surged from his knees towards her, a fire igniting in his eyes. 'Did Hugo ever hurt you because of me?'

His rage burned like molten metal, thick and scorching. Not at her, but *for* her. She shook her head.

'No. But I thought if I told him about the baby, he might have done something.'

'There is nothing he could have done to you because I *would* have come for you.'

'You were another country away. He had all the power. And by the time I thought I could say something it was all over, so I kept it to myself because you didn't need to suffer this pain.'

Yet as much as the ache now always lived

inside her, it felt good to share. To finally acknowledge with another person that their little boy had lived, if only for a short time.

'I'm suffering it now,' Gage said, his voice as cracked and broken as her heart. He flicked through more of the material till he found an old, faded photograph of her, holding their little boy all swaddled and hidden. The pain, raw on her face. Her midwife had said it would help, one day, to have this photo. That at some time in the future she'd want these memories.

'You've carried this case around since then,' he said.

'I carry it everywhere. It's always with me.'

Gage hunched over the papers as if curling into himself. The photograph dropped from his fingers and fell to the floor. He buried his head in his hands as his shoulders shuddered. He uttered no sound, but she knew his pain. She'd carried it around with her for too long. Six birthdays, six Mother's Days. Every milestone she should have been celebrating with their child, lost to her.

She draped herself over Gage's trembling body. Wrapped her arms around his shoulders and let the years of unshed tears fall. *Finally,* there was someone who knew. Another person who could mark the date as it passed. And as they clung on to each other a selfish, wicked thought grabbed hard at her like a kudzu vine and wouldn't let go. What if she could have Gage after all these years? But wanting was a dangerous thing. She still had secrets to keep, though holding them back now felt like trying to stop sand running through an hourglass.

It just ran through her fingers instead.

CHAPTER TEN

THIS PLACE HELD too many memories of his failures and regrets, and those regrets almost crushed Gage now. The pain in his chest wouldn't go away, a tearing, cutting kind of agony. He wondered if it ever would. All the things he and Eve had missed together threatened to slice him to pieces. The child lost to them both. He didn't know how Eve had dealt with it on her own, away from any support. How it didn't crush her now.

What if he'd ignored her cruel words seven years ago, had followed her across the world and fought for the woman he loved rather than giving up and wallowing in self-indulgence over her rejection? They could have been a family or, even if things had still turned out badly with their baby, they would have had each other to cling to. Instead, Eve had suffered in a foreign country. Alone.

Her weight lifted from his back, where she'd

held onto him and poured out her grief along with his. He couldn't understand how she could forgive what he never would—the end of everything they'd hoped for. He took a deep breath against the sadness that threatened to overwhelm him. He'd never forget what had been done by Eve's family. If he had to maintain the rage for both of them, then so be it. It was bright and hot enough to consume the grief of a thousand people and still have room to devour more.

He straightened up to look at Eve, her beautiful face marred by tears, blotchy and red. He gritted his teeth. 'Hugo *will* pay. For it all. If it's the last thing I do with my last breath, he'll know the meaning of suffering. A lifetime of it isn't enough for what he's done. Where is he now? Because, God help him, a reckoning is coming.'

Her eyes widened and she paled to the colour of parchment. The ruins of her mascara stood out as dark, wet tracks under her swollen eyes. She shook her head. 'No.'

'*No?*' Gage stood and began to pace. She was still defending him, after all that man had done?

'If you go to see him, what will you do?' Her voice trembled and choked as she stayed on her knees, as if begging him to stop what he never would. *Ever.* 'What will it achieve?'

He wheeled round. How could she not see? Her family, her *father* had destroyed their lives. Tainted the last seven years with his special brand of poison.

'I want to show him that he's lost, and I have it *all.* His company, and especially what he tried to keep from me. *You.*'

Eve scrambled to her feet. 'So I'm still being used as a weapon?'

She was talking in riddles.

'What the hell do you mean?'

'There's a future that holds love, not this hatred.' She clasped her hands in front of her. 'My father will reap his reward. There's nothing you can do to him that will make him unhappier than he is now, than he has been for most of his adult life.'

He shook his head, unbelieving. How she could even acknowledge Hugo after all that had gone before was unfathomable. 'You're protecting him?'

She shook her head, eyes wide. 'I'm protecting *you.* That's why I won't let you go.'

'You can't stop me.' He snatched his phone

from his pocket, called for a car. 'Tell me where he is, or I'll find him on my own. He'll know what he did!'

His ride would be here in under ten minutes. So little time and too much, when he wanted to rush out and tear her father's world apart, like he'd done to theirs. Gage paced the carpet, unable to stop because if he did, he feared he might fall and never get up. Eve didn't move. How could she be so still? With her arms now wrapped tightly around her waist, biting into her lower lip. Then she reached out, grabbed his arm and he had no choice but to stand there, forcing himself to stay upright.

'Gage, *please.*' Eve's grip was tight and strong for such slender fingers, her voice a bare tremor in the otherwise brutal silence of the room. 'You can't go… There are things you need to know… The truth of why I ended…us.'

The answer to the questions he'd asked for seven years hung just out of reach. Now nothing would get him to move from the spot in which he stood. Yet Eve seemed frozen, her eyes wide and pupils mere pinpricks. A pulse thrashed wildly at the base of her throat, as if they were on the edge of something too big to be knowable.

If anyone were to break the inertia, it would have to be him.

'What?'

The word jolted like a shock through Eve. She pulled her hand back as if he'd burned her. Now she was the one to pace, hands fluttering restlessly as she spoke.

'You've got to understand. At the time he said things were bad with Caron and that if he told everyone what he knew, it might fold. You love your parents. I didn't want you hurt like that.'

And still she didn't make sense. None of this did, her defence of Hugo. *Nothing.* 'What the hell are you talking about?'

'I can't... I have to...' She stopped. Her chest heaved as if every breath was an effort. Her eyes spilled over with tears. He almost moved to hold her up, because now it was as if she was the one who might fall. 'You need to know. Your father... Gus...is not your father.'

Everything froze, like the room had been hit by an ice storm.

'Chevaliers are charlatans and cheats, never to be trusted.'

His dad's words screamed in his ears. Gage shook his head, pointed at her, punctuating the air with his finger.

'No. You're lying.' Eve reared back like she'd been struck. 'It's not true. It's—'

'You need to talk to your mom and dad. Why would I lie?' Her hands were stretched out, as if imploring him to believe her when what she said was unbelievable. 'I've seen the evidence. My father said if I didn't end things, he'd tell everyone you weren't Gus's son. Better you hated me than you lost everything. I had to do it. To protect you.'

Gage shook his head. It couldn't be true. He was a Caron. Gus was his dad.

'Doesn't wash, *cher*. How were you going to explain us to your daddy now? That promise you demanded he keep was worthless with us together.'

Though only hours ago if Eve had told him she'd had a baby, he might not have believed that either...

'I thought we'd be done by the time my father recovered, if he did... Then things changed...' She tortured the sapphire ring on her finger, twisting it back and forth. Staring at the gleaming gems. It hit him so hard it felt like the breath had been almost knocked from his lungs. Those questions he'd asked of his parents when he'd been a child. How he didn't really look like his dad. The dread of realisation frosted over him because in the end, here was the perfect explanation for Eve's cruelty, the only one that made sense.

He'd been going to confront her father, and Eve knew Hugo would tell him what she'd kept hidden all these years.

Gus Caron was *not* his father.

That knowledge now fired the burn inside, a blinding realisation of all the lies told and toxic secrets kept.

'If your daddy had died you'd have kept this secret, wouldn't you?' he hissed. 'When I *deserved* to know.'

She walked up to him, a tentativeness about her as if she was approaching a wild animal. Maybe that's exactly what he was. The feral desire to lash out and hurt those he loved bit down hard. He barely held it in check because he knew only too well that words, once spoken, couldn't be unsaid.

'You did need to know but it wasn't my story

to tell and it should never have been told to you in hatred. The story needed to be told to you in love, by your parents. I—I was going to talk to them. Ask them to speak to you, and then...'

She looked at all the papers and scrapbooks lying in a scattered mess across the floor, like their dreams. Nothing could ever be the same after today. His world had ended and he wasn't sure how to start living again.

'So I'm not a Caron.' Gage turned his back on her. Walked away towards the window with fists clenched. Looked out at the view of a city he now loathed. 'It's too late now. This. Everything.'

He'd been a father, and hadn't known it. He was a bastard, and hadn't known that either. Nothing seemed stable anymore, like the ground had cracked beneath his feet. He dropped his head and looked at the floor to make sure it was solid because it felt like it would open up and swallow him whole. The hair on the back of his neck pricked, warning of someone close. Then there was a gentle press of a palm, which he supposed was meant to comfort, but instead it felt like a stab in the back. Just one more knife in the multitude that had struck there and stuck, leaving him permanently wounded.

'So much that's happened has been so wrong, but we can make it right. There's a future and we can—'

Gage wheeled round, and Eve took a step back. What could she see on his face that made her want to give him space? Not even he could read the emotions now churning inside him bar one. An endless hatred, focussed laser bright on one man.

'Your father deserves to be punished, and I will *relish* meting it out to him.'

Eve looked up at him, those blue eyes of hers so pale and sad. He wondered when he'd become inured to all the grief.

'And what happens when you're done with that? What then?'

He frowned. What did she mean? He'd triumph, that's what would happen.

'Then it'll be over.'

'Do you have any idea how to live a life where revenge isn't part of it?' She held out her hand and placed it on the centre of his chest, where his heart should be beating. He wasn't sure it was anymore. 'When will it ever be enough?'

The answer rang clear: it would *never* be enough, not for him. 'How can you let this go? He stole everything from us.'

'I don't care about that man. I can't control what he does, only what I feel. All I care about is you. Trust me, this will eat away at you like it's done to him.'

The heat of her palm burned into him, a reminder of how cold he'd become.

'I'm *not* your father.'

'No. Not now. But one day, if you keep going, you will be. What if my father's gone? I'm his daughter. Will you end up hating me too? This needs to stop.'

He moved away from Eve with her imploring eyes and gentle hands. Softer emotions had no place here, not in this room where all his hope had been smashed and broken. 'It'll stop when I say it does, or your father's in the grave.'

Eve clenched her fists by her sides. 'He could live another twenty years, and you want to carry on hating him for that long?'

He'd never stop. 'I'll loathe him till I'm in the grave myself.'

Her tears fell again, slipping down her cheeks, tracking down her pale skin. There'd been so many tears today they could have filled rivers with them. Eve wiped at her face, took a deep breath. Stood firm and proud.

'I have loved you for almost my whole life. I will continue to love you all the days I have left,' she said, taking the engagement ring from her finger and holding it out to him. For a moment he had trouble understanding what it all meant. 'But I can't do this anymore. I won't allow hatred to rule my life or infect another day.'

He stared at the ring for a few moments, then looked back at her. There was no way she would walk away from him, not now, not after everything. Not with so much left unfinished.

'We have a deal, and you're breaking it? If you don't carry this through to the end—'

'Then you'll what? Destroy me too?' She didn't look angry, she didn't look sad, just worn down and tired. Like someone had carved out all the vibrant parts of her and left a pale husk behind. 'I beg you, try your hardest because *nothing* could hurt me much more than I'm hurting now. I'll keep to our deal. You want to wheel me out as your fake fiancée for Greta Bonitz or anyone else? Fine. But us? We're done. Because your hatred for my father is stronger than your love for me, and I deserve more than that. I deserve *everything*.'

Her voice cracked and broke. She turned around, placed the ring on the side table and walked out the door, leaving all his dreams a tattered ruin in her wake.

CHAPTER ELEVEN

GAGE DROVE HIS rental car through the iron gates of his parents' home, roaring up the long drive past flowering hedges. He'd learned to ride a bicycle on this drive when he was five. His dad had taught him. Wobbling on training wheels with Gus always at his side, murmuring encouragement. The day those wheels had come off, he'd pedalled recklessly down to the end, the breeze whistling in his ears and his dad whooping and cheering after him.

His hands gripped the steering wheel hard. He parked the car, wrenched the door open and hurled himself out, slamming the door behind him. No, not his dad. Had both of his parents kept the secret, or was Gus ignorant? It was as if the people he'd loved his whole life, were now strangers to him.

He stood outside the front doors of his family home and looked up at the expansive portico above. When he'd been younger he'd seen this place as his heritage. All lies. His world was steeped in them so deeply he couldn't see the truth for the darkness anymore. Couldn't see any way out as everything he'd believed and known crumbled around him.

For so many years, he'd thought he'd known the enemy. Eve. Visions of her demanding better. Handing back the ring. Walking with her head held high out the door, that was a gaping wound he was sure would never heal. Yet again she'd left him. But she'd only been a bit player in this game, and he couldn't process that pain right now. His enemies had turned out to be closer to home. The one place he'd believed he was safe from lies and it turned out even here truth was lacking.

What was left for him now? He'd been conducting this quest for revenge on behalf of a family that wasn't even his. Every foundation he'd built his life on was an illusion. He didn't even know *who* he was.

He grabbed his keys to the house and opened the front door. Maybe he should give them back, since it didn't feel he had any rights here. This place had once been the happiest of homes. That had changed when Eve had left, the estate containing too many memories of her presence, so he rarely visited. Now he wondered whether there was reason to visit ever again.

His father would likely be in the den, so Gage made his way there, everything passing by in an amorphous blur. He was an imposter, with no place here. As he walked, he tamped down the sensation that grabbed his throat and squeezed till he reached the doorway. There the choking feeling increased till there was hardly enough air to fill his lungs. The man he'd once believed to be his father, a man he'd looked up to and admired as honest and good in a world full of fakes, glanced up, saw him. A smile broke out on his face as he stood.

'Gage! What are you doing here? We weren't expecting you.' His father looked happy after his break away. A prelude to retirement and handing over the reins of a company Gage wasn't sure he wanted any longer. Then the smile stuttered, died. Replaced by the tight mask of disapproval unvoiced. 'Is Eve with you?'

The wound in his heart opened and bled a little more. While this place held too many memories, his parents had been the bedrock of his life. He'd always pitied Eve's family and the conditional love she'd been shown. Now all he could do was stare.

He wasn't this man's child. If that dirty secret hadn't been kept, he and Eve could have been together. All that had gone before came down to this. His family's secrets and lies were the cause. His father, because he didn't know what else to call him, frowned.

'Son. What's wrong? Are the Chevaliers causing trouble? Has Eve…?'

He could hear the unfinished sentence. *Has Eve left you again*? How could he say what was wrong when everything was now over? It was too much to articulate. Eve had gone. He didn't know who the people who he'd once called his parents were anymore. His whole world had shifted and tilted, as if he'd woken up in an alternate dimension.

'I'm not your son, am I?'

He didn't know how he got the words out. They cut at his throat like ground glass. His father paled.

'What do you mean?' For a few moments Gage almost hoped that his father didn't know. That at least one of his parents hadn't been part of the duplicity. But the man who had always looked him straight in the eye now wouldn't meet his gaze.

'I'm. Not. Your. Son.'

Gus's legs gave way and he fell back into the leather chair. He buried his face in his hands. After a few moments he looked up at Gage, eyes moist with tears.

'How did you find out?'

Gage shut his own eyes for a moment as the words struck him with the force of a blow. Gus could not have hurt him more if he'd hit him. A punch would have been preferable.

'Does it matter?'

The final conversation with Eve screamed loudly in his ears. Then her rejection. Nothing mattered, with his world collapsing around him.

'No. It doesn't. Because you have always been my son.' The lines on Gus's face were etched deeper now, like his father had aged twenty years in a matter of moments. Gone was the strong man, the head of their small family. This man was a ghost. 'You were my son the day you were born.'

Gage shook his head, stabbed his finger at the air in front of him. 'But you're not my father.'

Gus flinched. Stood again. Walked out from

behind the old oak desk that Gage had once been destined to inherit. 'I took you fishing for bass. I taught you how to cast. We went to Little League together. I was with you every step as you pieced back together the heart a damned Chevalier shredded. I loved you then. I still love you, and you will *always* be my son.'

They sounded like fine words, but now it was all just a charade. His father glanced over his shoulder, a crease forming between his brows, pain written all over his face. Pain he'd last seen when Gus had bailed him out of a jail cell with a broken nose and terror in his heart. Pain Gage didn't give a damn about right now.

Let them all suffer. Let it all burn.

'Darling, it's lovely to see you...' His shoulders sagged. His mom. At least he knew one parent here was his. Gage didn't turn to look at her. She'd hidden as much from him as the man in front of him had.

'Betty, he knows.'

His mom stepped forward into his peripheral vision and grabbed the back of the chair in front of her.

'Darling.' Her voice was the barest of whispers. 'Please understand...'

He didn't want to hear. In this room the lies were the cause of all his hurts.

'There's nothing to understand, *Mom*. You lied to me. That man...' He pointed to the man who'd raised him. Whom he'd once loved. 'That man is not my father.'

Gus Caron looked at him. Stricken. His colour was grey. Gage didn't care. The pain on his parents' faces could never match the pain that was tearing him in two.

'Betty. This is a conversation I need to have with my boy.'

'I... I'll get some iced tea.'

'No. I think we need something stronger.'

'Then I'll leave you to talk.' His mother looked at him, tears dripping down her cheeks, before she left the room. He'd made a woman he loved cry, yet again. His father walked to a sideboard, grabbed a bottle and held it up.

'Want some?'

Gage shook his head. Gus poured himself a three-finger slug and his father was not a drinker.

'Hiding this from you was never planned. It just...never seemed a good time to say anything.'

Gage gritted his teeth so hard he thought they might crack. 'I asked you when I was nine why I didn't look like you. You both said I took after Mom's family.'

'You need to understand—'

'You all keep saying that and I've tried, but I'm out of ideas. Why don't you explain it to me? Because you've had *thirty* years!'

Gus gulped down half his drink. Winced. 'We were overjoyed to have you. And it didn't seem to matter. You were all your mother and I wanted. We tried to have children when we first got married. We couldn't. There was a problem with me.'

Gage had a small, sharp moment of bright hope, a shard that inserted itself and stuck. 'So you used a sperm donor?'

His father shook his head and that hope was dashed.

'You know your mom and I married young. It was one of the *many* reasons we were so against you and Eve, but especially given what happened to us... Marriage. It isn't easy. Which is something you'll learn with Eve if... But you're both older. Better able to deal with what will come your way.'

Gage looked down at his hands, gripping the leather seat back of the chair he stood behind. His nails cut into it. There was no relationship anymore. He and Eve were done. He held on even harder, because it felt right now like he was bleeding out all over the floor.

'We tried for so long to have a baby. Everything failed. Doctors said there was no explanation. Just one of those things. *Idiopathic infertility.*'

His father twirled the crystal tumbler in his hands. Took another mouthful of liquor.

'We weren't happy, son. Things were going wrong. And your mother and I, we both sought to ease our pain elsewhere.'

Gage rubbed his hands over his face. For as long as he'd been alive his parents had loved each other. He'd thought their marriage had been perfect. They had been an immutable force and now this? He shook his head. 'I don't want to know.'

'You're an adult and you need to hear this. It's where it starts. Your mom fell pregnant. It wasn't planned. It just happened. She didn't want to be with the father. He didn't want her either.'

'Who is he? Do I know him? Did he know about me?'

'Yes, he knew about you. No, you don't know him. I can give you his name. He's a business-man in California with a wife and two grown kids of his own. A whole lot of folks made a whole bunch of mistakes back then and in the end he didn't want to be in your life. Your mom and I had a choice to make. We wanted children. And here was our chance.'

Gage couldn't stand any longer. He pulled out the chair he'd been holding onto and sat, trembling. He regretted refusing his father's offer, wanting a drink of whiskey now himself to numb the feelings that rioted inside him. 'I wasn't a commodity.'

'No. You were our greatest success and greatest love. And yet you were a product of our greatest failings. Neither your mom nor I were innocent in this thing. In the end we had to fight hard for our marriage, and we succeeded. You're a blessing. I didn't care who your biological father was. I'd been no prince myself and it would have been hypocritical of me to criticise your mom for failing when I had first, and more than once. It wasn't easy fixing our marriage.

Both of us had a great deal to forgive the other for. The easy thing was always you. From the moment you were born you were my son. You were no one else's.'

'How did you do it? How did you forgive her?'

His father downed the last of his glass, sat back in his chair. Looked at him with soft warmth in his clear brown eyes. A look that had once been familiar and was now strange and confusing.

'While saving the marriage was one of the hardest things I've done, in the end forgiving was easy. I forgave your mom because I love her.'

Gage left the house, wandered through the sprawling gardens, down to the edge of the property, to where the large magnolia grew. He leaned against the trunk, sliding down to sit on the ground underneath. Not caring if he ruined his trousers in the tree's detritus, not caring about anything at all. He felt numb, broken by the revelations of the past few days.

About Eve leaving him.

He shook his head, refused to think about it, about her final words. Gage stared at the huge wall separating his parents' land from the Chevaliers'. From a vantage point in the branches above he used to watch Eve in the garden. He'd been lonely, an only child with not many friends to play with, and a bright little girl picking flowers hadn't seemed like the enemy but a possible friend.

To this day he still didn't know why the Carons and the Chevaliers held such enmity towards each other. It had been ingrained in his psyche for so long he hadn't questioned it. From imploring him never to go over the fence if he lost a ball or a paper plane there to the open hostility when they saw each other in public, he'd grown to accept something he should have fought, for Eve's sake and for his own. As children they hadn't embraced the hatred that had poisoned every interaction between their families. As young adults they'd naïvely thought they could end it. Until seven years ago when he'd believed he'd finally understood that a Chevalier could never be trusted. Turned out the people he shouldn't trust had been far closer to home.

More fool him for believing *anyone*.

Footsteps scuffed through the fallen leaves

surrounding him. He looked to his left, up at the pale, drawn face of his mom.

'Darling, I'm so sorry.'

He shrugged. What did it matter now? Apologies changed nothing. He was here. Eve was gone. His father wasn't his father. Nothing was right with the world as he knew it.

'At least you're my mother.'

'Do *not* say that to me. I understand you're angry. You have every right to be. But think.' She pointed up to the house, her voice trembling. 'That man has been *nothing* but your father since the day you were born.'

If he tried to intellectualise it, his mom was right. He couldn't fault Gus. Apart from how they looked and that one question when he'd been nine, he'd never guessed his dad was not his blood. The man had given him unflinching love and support, had bailed him out of jail when he'd been arrested after he and Eve had run. Paying lawyers to clear his name. Never, ever questioning what had led Gage to flee in the dead of night with the daughter of a sworn enemy. Nursing him through the hangovers and poor behaviour after Eve had told him never to speak to her again.

Other kids had always been envious of how much his dad loved him, including Eve. He'd always thought how lucky he'd been. He knew it, but that didn't stop the pain scouring through his veins like acid.

'Were you ever going to tell me?'

His mom sighed, sat down next to him in her pretty dress on the leaves and raw earth. She'd get dirty too and he wasn't sure why that worried him. His mom cupped his cheek. Her fingers were warm, but a tremor ran through them.

'I wish I could say we were bigger people. But no. Time passed and the harder it became till we wondered what the point would be. Then you told us you were engaged to Eve—'

Pain struck him straight to the heart. He rubbed his chest. 'You don't have to worry about that. We're not engaged now.'

The silence his words met flayed him some more. His parents' disapproval had been clear. It had needled in the beginning, even if the arrangement with Eve was a fake. But right now he couldn't bear to hear it. His mom took a deep breath.

'Oh, sweetheart. Why?'

The words caught in his throat. A tight lump

that he swallowed down before it choked him. 'She knew all along about me not being dad's son. Her father threatened to tell me if she didn't break it off all those years ago. She was pregnant. She lost the…'

He couldn't go on. The pain of it was too much. His mom wrapped him in her arms, like she'd done so many times when he'd been a child.

'I'm sorry,' she murmured into his hair. 'I know platitudes will never be enough. As adults, we have so *much* to beg Eve's and your forgiveness for. We've all failed you because we acted like children and couldn't let things go.'

He took a deep breath. 'She says I'm like her father.'

'You must have made her furious to use that insult.'

'I said and did things I'm not proud of.'

His mom patted him on the arm. 'That one statement tells me you're not like him, because you have the capacity to learn. Hugo Chevalier doesn't. He never did, which is one of the reasons I fell in love with your father. We may have had our problems. Serious problems. But your father could think and reason and he cared. He's the best of men, even with his human frailties. You take after him, not that man next door who only ever wanted to tear things apart.'

Gage looked up at his mom, the belief in what she saw written in the gentle smile on her face. 'You have so much faith in me.'

'Your father and I both do, darling. It's time you had faith in yourself.'

He didn't know what to do, how to fix this. All he knew was that he loved Eve, had never, ever stopped, and he wasn't sure how to tell her, how to forgive...either of them.

'There's one question I've never asked. Why do our families hate each other so much? How did it come to this?'

His mom looked at the fence separating the two properties then back to their home.

'That's a long story,' she said.

'Then tell me.' Gage leaned back against the trunk of the old tree. 'Seems I've got all the time in the world.'

CHAPTER TWELVE

EVE PUFFED OUT a breath, blowing at a strand of unruly curls that had fallen across her face. She wiped her hands on her dusty jeans and looked around at the packing boxes now filling her Paris apartment. She'd made a few hard choices after leaving Gage and America behind.

The agony of that decision still sliced right through her, stinging as fresh as a papercut, but she'd finally concluded that she deserved *more*. All her life she'd danced to the tune of others. She was tired of living the way everyone else expected, and now she'd had enough. This time was her own.

So she'd flown back to France, given notice that Knight needed to find another CEO for the French operation, and had walked away from it all. Putting hatred and anyone determined to hang onto it behind her. She'd seen the way that emotion destroyed. It had no place in her life anymore.

As soon as she packed up her possessions here, she'd move and start growing the plants she loved. A simple life worrying about the soil, sun and scent and nothing much else. At the same time she'd try to heal her broken heart, though she knew that there were some things from which she might never fully recover. Putting her heart back together was one, because some of the pieces were missing. They probably always had been.

But thoughts of heartbreak weren't going to get this apartment packed, and the drive to move and move forward was the only thing keeping her upright. Kitchen, she'd do that next. As Eve grabbed a box and began taping it, her intercom sounded. It was the apartment's concierge. She answered.

'Mademoiselle Chevalier, a delivery.'

She breathed out a sigh of relief. 'Thank you. Send them up.' The extra packing boxes she ordered. At a knock, she opened the door. Only it wasn't packing boxes, but two men, each holding a vase of flowers.

These weren't just any flowers either, but blowsy English roses in a riot of pinks and apricots. Perfect, rambunctious blooms spilling from their containers, filling the hall with a glorious scent.

Her heart throbbed as she gripped the hard wood of the door, frozen. Staring like a fool at the men, who were only trying to do their jobs. She shook herself out of her inertia, stood back and let them in, asking them to place the roses on the dining table and sideboard.

'Is there any card?' She didn't really need one. There was only one person who they could be from. A surge of emotion welled inside, threatening to break her. She bit her lip to tamp it down.

One of the men shrugged. *'Non.* Only flowers.'

They left and she moved to close the door but one of the men stopped her with a wry smile.

'There are more.'

She stood back as the flowers kept coming, filling her apartment. Magnificent vases were placed on every flat surface with roses bursting from them as she directed where they should go.

She looked around at all the colour overwhelming the space and realised it had never really been a home to her because it hadn't held all of her heart. Those missing pieces she'd left years ago with Gage. He'd always kept a part of her, always would. She wiped away a tear that threatened to fall. He wasn't her future. That was now a quiet, peaceful life. Let Gage and her father wage a war of revenge and attrition. Too much had been lost, and for what? She was sick of the game and the hand she kept being dealt, so she'd folded. Tossed her cards on the table and walked away.

The final vase was placed on a small side table, which looked like it would topple under the weight of the outrageous arrangement.

'Is that all?' she asked, looking around the room that seemed more like a florist's shop than an apartment now.

'Not quite.'

She stilled. That voice, the deep burr of it igniting a fire in her that would probably never go out. She whipped around.

Gage stood there in the doorway to her apartment, cradling in the crook of his arm a large bunch of purple and lavender roses wrapped in petal pink paper and Cellophane. He wore soft, faded jeans and a crumpled shirt. Stubble shadowed his angular jaw, his golden hair all messy, as if he'd raked through it with restless fingers.

It looked like he'd rolled out of bed, thrown on clothes left over from a long night before and run over here. But he couldn't have done that. Instead, he'd travelled halfway around the world. To see her.

Her traitorous heart skipped a few beats.

He was so beautiful it hurt. The way his worn clothes hugged the muscles of his strong body. The planes of his face more angular than she remembered. Honed. *Determined.* His blue eyes like the summer skies in Grasse that would always haunt her. She'd loved him her whole life, no matter how many times she'd lied to herself, trying to convince her wounded heart they'd never had a chance. Every part of her was attuned to him, even when they'd been apart.

It was something she had to come to terms with because he couldn't be the man she wanted. She needed to put the warring behind her. She deserved more than being a pawn on a chessboard built of loathing. The terrible thing was that Gage deserved more too but he wouldn't see it. She couldn't bear to witness the man she'd loved for most of her days becoming a slave to hatred, being eaten away by degrees.

'May I come in?' he asked, still standing outside the door, not even a toe over the threshold.

She somehow convinced her trembling legs to move and stood back, whilst he edged past. She shut the door with a soft snick behind her and he followed her into the lounge area.

'These are for you.' He held out the bouquet. She took it from him and buried her nose in the velvety petals, inhaling their scent. Lemon and raspberries.

'I think I probably have enough.'

'You can never have too many flowers.' He looked around the room, down at the floor, then his gaze rested on the packing boxes. 'You're moving. To Grasse.'

It wasn't a question. A jolt of surprise spiked through her. 'Is that an educated guess?'

Gage ran his hand through his hair. 'A large parcel of Caron shares has been sold. Your loan's been repaid. The farm is off the rental market and you've resigned as CEO. It's no guess.'

She put the flowers on a chair. They could go into water later, once she'd dealt with this and moved on, but tell that to her body, which vibrated at the impossible thrill of having him near, in her space. She cocked her head. 'You been keeping an eye on me?'

'Always.' Gage's voice ground out, wounded and raw. His throat convulsed in a swallow. 'I don't know how to look away.'

And there was the anguish of them, described in one sentence. Neither of them knew how to stop this. For days after she'd come here she'd barely been able to haul her sorry self out of bed each morning. It had been a struggle to simply put one foot in front of the other and not to scour the internet for any news about him. She'd wondered if she'd ever fully get over him and had resigned herself to that answer being 'No'. He would always be part of her. Even now, she craved to reach out, to touch him. To comfort and be comforted. To trace her hands over his strong arms. Arms where she'd once felt protected. Loved... And yet going back felt like an end, not a beginning.

Finally, someone had to say *enough*.

'Gage, what are you doing here?'

'I've come to talk. I've been so focussed on... what's gone wrong in my life.'

She planted her hands on her hips. 'You can say the word. It's *revenge*.' She'd been in denial for so long she refused to accept the same of him.

Gage nodded. 'You're right. I've been so focussed on *revenge* I lost sight of everything that might have been good.' He shoved his hands in the pockets of his jeans and for a moment looked like a chastened schoolboy. 'I've spoken to my parents.'

That conversation must have been awful. Her heart, which she was struggling to harden, softened a little further. 'I'm sorry to have been the one to tell you, but you needed to know. If only—'

'No.' Gage shook his head. 'There's no need to be sorry. In the end you were the only one with the courage to say anything. I'm glad it was you, and not Hugo.'

Something inside her unknotted a fraction because that final and terrible decision to say anything at all had tortured her, even though she'd known she'd had no choice. 'How did the conversation with your parents go?'

He shrugged. 'As well as can be expected when finding out the man you've loved as a father all your life, isn't your father. But I learned some things.'

He took a deep breath, looked at her with his summer-blue eyes. Her heart broke all over again every time she was close to him. No more. While it was a difficult habit to overcome, *she* was the priority now. She just had to stay strong.

'Did anyone ever tell you why our families hate each other?' he asked.

'"Carons are liars and thieves."' She repeated the words her family had tried to etch in her consciousness from birth.

Gage cocked his head. '"Chevaliers are charlatans and cheats."'

'Now we've established that, does any other reason matter?'

It didn't really. People had choices. You could move forward and get on with your life or you could wallow. Forward was the only direction for her now.

Yet with Gage here again in her home, surrounded by flowers, the idea of moving forward on her own didn't seem like a triumph. It seemed like a recipe for loneliness, because even when they weren't together, he'd always been her destination. She swallowed back the burn in her throat, the stinging in her nose.

'It matters. Because it's what led us here. It

matters because we can't move on unless we know how it began in the first place.' Gage took a step forward, flexing his fingers as if he wanted to touch her. She took a step back and steeled herself, when all she craved to do was tumble into his arms and forget warring families. His shoulders slumped for the briefest of moments then he straightened, like a warrior readying himself for battle, and began pacing.

'It started with a business deal between friends, and bringing the telegraph to Mississippi. Your family claimed mine had a side investment in the company supplying utility poles that wasn't disclosed to Chevalier. Mine say yours inflated quotes to skim the extra and make an outrageous profit at Caron's expense. The hatred grew from there. It waxed and waned over the years depending on which family was doing better. Those things aren't really a surprise.' He stopped tracking across the parquet floor, turned to her. 'Your dad being engaged to my mom is.'

'What?' Her legs almost folded under her. Luckily there was a couch close. She sat down hard, her hand to her chest as if that would somehow settle her pounding heart. 'That's… that's *impossible.*'

Gage remained standing. 'My mom said their parents knew each other, were old friends. An engagement between Mom and Hugo was expected. Then she met my dad. He'd come home from college for the holidays and it was love at first sight. They married young and your dad never forgave her. It caused a scandal at the time, given the rivalry between our families. Though I wouldn't be surprised if Gus secretly liked stealing Mom away from a Chevalier. But things only went nuclear again after Mom had me.'

Eve wrapped her arms around her waist. Gage's voice was distant and remote through the buzzing in her ears. She could put a few things together and the truth of them plunged like a knife and twisted. 'He always wanted a boy. He was jealous of what your mom and dad had. Two girls were never enough for him.'

'He was a fool. You are enough, *cher.*' His voice was soft and gentle. 'You're more than enough.'

Whatever the truth in Gage's words, the realisation still hurt. 'It's why he was so happy when he found out about you. It meant the dream he assumed was your parents' lives wasn't the fairy-tale he'd imagined.'

Gage walked forward, sat on the couch but as far away from her as he could, like he was giving her space to glue herself back together. It didn't matter. Another country was too close where he was concerned.

'Mom and Dad went through a really bad patch in their marriage. They almost broke up. Of the many reasons they objected to us, our being so young was one of the biggest. They wanted me to have lived my life, be older. Be sure.'

She picked at a loose thread on the knee of her old jeans, anything to resist the urge to close the space, crawl into his arms and never leave. 'I was sure then. The arrogance and innocence of my young self. I thought love would conquer everything. But we would have burned out.'

He shook his head. 'No. We wouldn't. I was sure back then too, and I'm even surer now.'

Her heart pounded a wild and desperate rhythm, crushing the breath right out of her. Hope was something she could not allow to spark, not now. Because that tiny pilot light of hope in the face of all the futility surrounding them had the power to burn her to ashes.

She was terrified of who might rise out of them.

'Gage, stop.'

He ran his hands through his hair again, some golden strands falling over his brow. It almost undid her, seeing this self-contained man so messy and rumpled, all because of her.

'Tell me you don't want me, and I'll walk out the door right now. But I never want you to live under the assumption I didn't love you. I did. I do. I have for years.' Gage turned his body to face her, his gaze steady and sure. 'I'll never stop.'

And it didn't matter what seemed sensible and rational and right. That hope burst to life in a bright, hot conflagration and all she could do was let herself burn.

Gage sat on the edge of the couch, that precarious position a metaphor for his life right now. All that he desired was in this room. There was no plan B for him. It was a case of either living his best life or merely existing. Eve looked away from him, at all the vases that decorated every surface. This gesture, grand as it appeared, wasn't enough. In all reality, probably nothing would be enough to earn her forgiveness for how he'd behaved.

She looked so beautiful and fragile sitting here, like the blooms that filled the room. One wrong breath, a careless touch and the petals would bruise and fall. It was all he could do not to reach out. To brush away the smudge of dust on her cheek. To kiss away the look of sorrow in her eyes, for which he was entirely responsible.

She shook her head. The crack in his heart widened a little more.

'But…you've got no room in your life for me. You want to destroy my family. Life's about living. Building things, not tearing them down.'

The look on her face almost broke him; the corners of her mouth trembling in a futile fight not to turn down. Her eyes were a little red, gleaming with tears he knew she refused to shed. He didn't deserve them anyhow. Didn't deserve her, but he couldn't leave without trying. In the end, all he wanted her to know was that she was loved.

'I was wrong. So wrong in so many ways. Pursuing Knight Enterprises like I did. Forcing you into this situation. They were the actions of a cruel man. You were right to accuse me of becoming like your father. Loving someone means letting them go and I should have done that. Instead, I treated love like a possession. But it's not. It's something bestowed not something you take and hoard. I love you, Eve, but I *will* walk away if that's what you need to be happy.'

Gage inched closer, close enough so their knees brushed. Even that hint of a touch sent shockwaves right through him. Eve didn't turn away, she didn't move at all. This close he could see the tired, dark circles under her eyes that she'd tried to conceal. They reflected his own. Both of them looked wretched.

She stared at where their knees barely touched, before looking at him. Her brows rose a fraction, eyes wide and blue, the question in them clear.

'Can you promise me no revenge?'

In the end that was the easy part. Getting her to trust him would be harder and he'd work at it for ever if he had to. Gage nodded.

'All I want is you. It's all I've ever wanted, I just didn't realise it.' He took her hands in his own. They were cool and the barest of tremors shivered through them. He hoped he could warm her, now and for ever. 'I'm so damned tired of looking for the worst in everything. I want to see the best, and you were always the best thing that had happened in my life. I should have trusted you and our love. If I'd come after you back then, rather than believing the lies, maybe things would have been different.'

She dropped her head, looked at their joined hands. 'You believed me when I was unspeakably cruel. I can hardly forgive myself for what I said to you because my father demanded it.'

'Your words were cruel, but I should have known they were a lie. I should have trusted you more.'

Eve squeezed his fingers, and Gage squeezed back, holding on tight.

'I should have fought for us instead of giving up,' she said.

'I wasn't worthy of you then. And I'm sure as hell not worthy of you now.'

'You were always worthy.' The threatened tears in Eve's eyes now brimmed and overflowed, tracking down her cheeks. 'If you weren't, I wouldn't have tried to protect you.'

He couldn't stand the distance anymore. He reached out to her and hauled her onto his lap. She didn't resist, nestling into him as he wrapped her tightly in his embrace. Closing his eyes and relishing the feel of her again, all soft and pliant. At that moment something about his upside-down world righted itself again.

'It was my job to protect *you*,' he said, murmuring into her unruly hair as it escaped from its tie. He stroked his hand over it, a marvel of twisted silk under his fingers. 'And I failed, in every way.'

'We were both young, neither of us knew what we were doing then.' Eve's fingers traced over his chest, stroking him like some overgrown cat. He could almost have purred at the pleasure of her tentative touches, as if learning him all over again. 'All I know is that I can't live with hate. I want to surround myself with love.'

'You'll have it every day, *cher*. That's one thing I can promise.'

Her hands left his chest, moved to his face and drifted to stroke the bridge of his nose, under his right eye, the places where he carried the scars of that terrible night seven years earlier.

'I'm sorry for these. For my father.'

'I earned them, loving you. You have nothing to apologise for.' It was all he could do not to take her face in his hands, to kiss her. But he held back. There was more that needed to be said. Building a solid foundation for the future he craved, one with Eve as his wife. 'Do you want some company growing your roses?'

She pulled back, looked up at him. 'Don't you have an international conglomerate to run?'

He shrugged. 'I can do that from wherever there's an internet connection. What I want more is you. And I'll be wherever you are. I'll do whatever you need. We'd always planned on making a home like the house in Grasse.'

'So dreams can come true?' Eve's eyes were wide and questioning. He didn't want to make her question, he wanted to be her every answer.

'I think we've spent our lives apart preparing to come back to each other, even if we didn't realise it. So now I want to make our engagement real. To marry you, like we planned once. Does that fit in with your dreams?'

The flicker of her pulse beat strong and solid at the base of her throat. He'd kiss there first, if she let him. When she said yes. For now, holding her, being allowed to love her was enough.

Eve plucked at something on his shirt, gave a light, tremulous laugh. 'Working out place settings for guests at the reception would be a nightmare. Maybe we should elope.'

He placed his fingers under her chin and tilted her face so she'd look at him again. Her eyes were tight, wary. He hated that uncertainty there, the things family enmity had forced upon them. 'You will be the most beautiful bride and I want to see it. It's what I always wanted for you. In whatever dress you've dreamed of, at the wedding you deserve. Nothing less.'

'I never cared about that.' She slid her arms around his neck, threading her fingers into his hair. He relished each touch, caress as a gift of trust. He hoped he could prove himself to her so she'd never doubt anything again. 'All I wanted was you.'

That was the last bit of encouragement he needed. Gage made sure his hold on Eve was secure and stood, cradling her in his arms. She squeaked in surprise but her body didn't tense, as if she was confident of him at last, and that was his promise to this amazing woman. He'd never let her down or let her fall. Ever again.

'You've got me, you always have. But I need to grab something out of my pocket.'

She pouted, tightened her arms around his neck a fraction. He almost gave up on what he'd planned to do. They could find the bedroom instead, stay there all day. Then they could finish packing and move. Together. He wouldn't leave her alone again. But this time he was determined to do it right. To make up in a small way for generations of wrongs. He loosened his grip and she sighed, untangling herself from him and sliding down his body as he bit back a moan.

Gage reached into his pocket, pulled out the glittering engagement ring and held it up. At the time he'd bought it, all he'd been looking for had been something large and valuable. A message to the world and nothing to the woman who would wear it. Until he'd seen this ring, and then all he'd been able to think of was her.

'Our dreams start today. Simple, wild, whatever you want we'll make them true together.'

Eve placed her right hand over his heart, which pounded under her palm. 'My knight in shining armour.'

She smiled, wide and bright. There were tears

in her eyes but he knew those were tears of joy. He'd do all he could to never see her cry tears of sadness again.

'Or piratical marauder. I can be either. I can be everything you want and anyone you need.'

Eve's smile turned sultry, her pupils huge, dark caverns in the pale blue. Soon he'd explore everything that wicked mind of hers was conjuring up. Now they had all the time in the world.

'You already are,' she said, her voice low and soft.

He closed his eyes for a moment. Thanking the heavens for this, for her. For second chances. 'Marry me, Eve. We both deserve a happy ending and I'll fight every day to ensure you get it.'

'Yes,' she said, and the power of their love filled him with its warmth as he slipped the ring on her finger. 'There's nothing in the whole world that would make me happier than that.'

EPILOGUE

Later

EVE LAY BACK in Gage's arms on the couch, his fingers tracing along a fine chain round her neck where her wedding and engagement rings lay. It had been a few months now since they'd fitted her fingers. Warmth flooded over her at his gentle caress. He plucked the chain, lifting it so the rings dangled in front of her, swaying back and forth.

'Happy anniversary, Mrs Caron,' he murmured. She loved the sound of those words on his lips. Her dreams spun into a perfect reality with that sentence.

'Two blissful years, Mr Caron.'

She hadn't realised how wrong everything had been until they'd married. Now all seemed right with the world. As if she'd found the last piece of a puzzle, finally fitting it into place. Their wedding had been everything she'd dreamed of, and more. Her dress a confection of antique lace and tulle. Blooms crowning her head as they'd been married surrounded by the flowers of her farm. Roses, lavender, jasmine. Such magic had infused those moments after they'd said their vows, she'd felt like a fairy princess marrying her prince. A day so full of joy she hadn't stopped smiling since.

Even the absence of her family hadn't dented her happiness. They'd made their choices, she'd made hers. She'd promised herself two years ago that the only direction she'd look was forward. With Gage as her husband, it was an easy promise to keep because he was right there with her, supporting her at every step.

Eve reached her arm behind her, running her fingers through Gage's hair as he allowed the rings to nestle back against her chest. She turned her head and he lowered his, capturing her lips in a gentle, lingering kiss.

'You were the most beautiful bride.' His hands slid over her large and still-increasing belly. 'Even more beautiful now. How's our little bean doing in there?'

Eve laughed.

'She's not little anymore, and *definitely* not a *bean*.' Eve shifted to get comfortable then settled again into Gage's embrace. They enjoyed lazing here in the Paris apartment they'd moved back to as her pregnancy had progressed, to be close to the hospital where she'd deliver their baby any day now. As she relaxed, a tell-tale jab struck her near the ribs. 'There! She did it again. Did you feel?'

'Yeah.' She adored the sound of wonder in Gage's voice at their baby's kick. His excitement over every moment of her pregnancy was infectious. Marvelling at the changes in her body, even her swollen fingers and ankles. He rubbed where their baby's foot pressed against his hand. 'Things getting a bit tight in there?'

She smiled. 'Are you trying to say that I'm ripe?'

Gage slid his hand over her stomach, up her arms. The tip of a finger drifted across her collarbone. She closed her eyes, relishing the pleasure of his caress.

'Like a peach. I just want to take a bite.' He dropped his lips to her ear and grazed his teeth over the shell of it, his breath feathering her skin. Goose-bumps shivered down her arms. 'I adore your curves.'

'I adore you,' she said. Their love had grown, expanded. Filling all the holes left behind by grief and loss. There was simply no room for sadness anymore. 'When are your mom and dad planning to come?'

It hadn't taken long for Gage to reframe his family's past, present and future. In a more contemplative moment he'd admitted Gus Caron was exactly the man he would have wanted as a father, if given the choice. And from then on Gus became 'Dad' again.

'A couple of weeks after our little girl arrives, so they say. I'm betting on earlier. How about your sister—have you convinced her to visit?'

Veronique had reached out after the wedding photos had hit the press with a simple text.

You've never looked happier.

The steps to communicating had been tentative, but that was okay. They had all the time in the world.

'She's trying not to show it but she's crazy excited to be an aunty. I'm betting about a day after you send her the first picture, she'll be right on a plane, claiming her status.'

Gage groaned. 'Remind me to delay the photos a bit or the house is going to get crowded.'

'Even if you do, they'll be beating down our door anyhow. There are a lot of people excited about this baby.'

Gage placed a hand over hers, threaded his fingers through her own.

'Call me selfish, but I want a little time to introduce myself to our daughter. To get to know her. Have her get to know us...' His voice caught. Sometimes emotion overcame them both. The excitement, the joy. And for Gage the fierce need to protect.

That was fine, because she protected him right back. She squeezed his fingers. 'Your daughter will love you just as much as I do. Even more than you love her. I promise.'

'I know. You showed me the way, reminding me *how* to love. I'm so full of it there's no room for anything else.' He lifted their joined hands and pressed hers to his mouth. 'I've loved you my whole life, *cher.*'

The words she'd said to him, the words they'd written into their wedding vows. Their promise to one another. Words of love that filled every day of their lives, now and for ever.

She turned to him and smiled. 'And I'll continue to love you all the days I have left.'

* * * * *

LET'S TALK
Romance

For exclusive extracts, competitions
and special offers, find us online:

f facebook.com/millsandboon

⬤ @millsandboonuk

🐦 @millsandboon

Or get in touch on 0844 844 1351*

For all the latest titles coming soon,
visit millsandboon.co.uk/nextmonth

*Calls cost 7p per minute plus your phone company's price per
minute access charge

Want even more
ROMANCE?

Join our bookclub today!

'Mills & Boon books, the perfect way to escape for an hour or so.'

Miss W. Dyer

'Excellent service, promptly delivered and very good subscription choices.'

Miss A. Pearson

'You get fantastic special offers and the chance to get books before they hit the shops'

Mrs V. Hall